A TEMPESTUOUS TEMPTATION

BY

CATHY WILLIAMS

MILLS & BOON

First published in Great Britain 2012
by Mills & Boon, an imprint of Harlequin (UK) Limited.
Large Print edition 2013
Harlequin (UK) Limited, Eton House,
18-24 Paradise Road, Richmond, Surrey TW9 1SR

© Cathy Williams 2012

ISBN: 978 0 263 23168 7

Harlequin (UK) policy is to use papers that are natural,
renewable and recyclable products and made from
wood grown in sustainable forests. The logging and
manufacturing process conform to the legal environmental
regulations of the country of origin.

Printed and bound in Great Britain
by CPI Antony Rowe, Chippenham, Wiltshire

CHAPTER ONE

LUIZ Carlos Montes looked down at the slip of paper in his hand, reconfirmed that he was at the correct address and then, from the comfort of his sleek, black sports car, he briefly scanned the house and its surroundings. His immediate thought was that this was not what he had been expecting. His second thought was that it had been a mistake to drive his car here. The impression he was getting was that this was the sort of place where anything of any value that could be stolen, damaged or vandalised just for the hell of it would be.

The small terraced house, lit by the street lamp, fought a losing battle to maintain some level of attractiveness next to its less palatable neighbours. The tidy pocket-sized front garden was flanked on its left side by a cement square on which dustbins were laid out in no particular order, and on its right by a similar cement square where a rusted car languished on blocks, awaiting attention. Further along was a parade of shops comprised of a Chinese takeaway, a sub-post office, a hairdresser, an off-licence and a newsagent which seemed to be a meeting point for just the sort of youths whom Luiz suspected would not hesitate to zero in on his car the second he left it.

Fortunately he felt no apprehension as he glanced at the group of hooded teenagers smoking in a group outside the off-licence. He was six-foot-three with a muscled body that was honed to perfection thanks to a rigorous routine of exercise and sport when he could find the time. He was more than capable of putting the fear of God into any group of indolent cigarette-smoking teenagers.

But, hell, this was still the last thing he needed. On a Friday evening. In December. With the threat of snow in the air and a shedload of emails needing his attention before the whole world went to sleep for the Christmas period.

But family duty was, in the end, family duty and what choice had he had? Having seen this dump for himself, he also had to concede that his mission, inconvenient though it might be, was a necessary one.

He exhaled impatiently and swung out of the car. It was a bitterly cold night, even in London. The past week had been characterised by hard overnight frosts that had barely thawed during the day. There was a glittery coating over the rusting car in the garden next to the house and on the lids of the bins in the garden to the other side. The smell of Chinese food wafted towards him and he frowned with distaste.

This was the sort of district into which Luiz never ventured. He had no need to. The faster he could sort this whole mess out and clear out of the place, the better, as far as he was concerned.

With that in mind, he pressed the doorbell and kept his finger on it until he could hear the sound of footsteps scurrying towards the front door.

On the verge of digging into her dinner, Aggie heard the sound of the doorbell and was tempted to ignore it, not least because she had an inkling of an idea as to whose finger was on it. Mr Cholmsey, her landlord, had been making warning noises about the rent, which was overdue.

'But I always pay on time!' Aggie had protested when he had telephoned her the day before. 'And I'm only overdue by *two days*. It's not my fault that there's a postal strike!'

Apparently, though, it was. He had been kind enough to 'do her the favour' of letting her pay by cheque when *all his other tenants* paid by direct debit... And *look where it got him...*it just *wasn't good enough...* People were queuing for that house...he could rent it to a more reliable tenant *in a minute...*

If the cheque wasn't with him *by the following day*, he would have to have cash from her.

She had never actually met Mr Cholmsey. Eighteen months ago, she had found the house through an agency and everything had been absolutely fine—until Mr Cholmsey had decided that he could cut out the middle man and handle his own properties. Since then, Alfred Cholmsey had been an ongoing headache, prone to ignoring requests for things to be fixed and fond of reminding her how scarce rentable properties were in London.

If she ignored the summons at the door, she had

no doubt that he would find some way of breaking the lease and chucking her out.

Keeping the latch on, she cautiously opened the door a crack and peered out into the darkness.

'I'm really sorry, Mr Cholmsey...' She burst into speech, determined to get her point of view across before her disagreeable, hateful landlord could launch his verbal attack. 'The cheque should have arrived by now. I'll cancel it and make sure that I have the cash for you tomorrow. I promise.' She wished the wretched man would do her the courtesy of at least standing in her very reduced line of vision instead of skulking to the side, but there was no way that she was going to pull open the door. You could never be too careful in this neighbourhood.

'Who the hell is Mr Cholmsey, and what are you talking about? Just open the door, Agatha!'

That voice, that distinctive, *loathsome* voice, was so unexpected that Aggie suddenly felt the need to pass out. What was Luiz Montes doing here? On her doorstep? *Invading her privacy?* Wasn't it bad enough that she and her brother had been held up for inspection by him over the past eight months? Verbally poked and prodded under the very thin guise of hospitality and 'just getting to know my niece's boyfriend and his family'. Asked intrusive questions which they had been forced to skirt around and generally treated with the sort of suspicion reserved for criminals out on parole.

'What are *you* doing here?'

'Just open the door! I'm not having a conversation with you on your doorstep!' Luiz didn't have to struggle to imagine what her expression would be. He had met her sufficient times with her brother and his niece to realise that she disapproved of everything he stood for and everything he said. She'd challenged him on every point he made. She was defensive, argumentative and pretty much everything he would have made an effort to avoid in a woman.

As he had told himself on numerous occasions, there was no way he would ever have subjected himself to her company had he not been placed, by his sister who lived in Brazil, in the unenviable position of having to take an interest in his niece and the man she had decided to take up with. The Montes family was worth an untold fortune. Checking out the guy his niece was dating was a simple precaution, Luisa had stressed. And, while Luiz couldn't see the point because the relationship was certain to crash and burn in due course, his sister had insisted. Knowing his sister as well as he did, he had taken the path of least resistance and agreed to keep a watchful eye on Mark Collins, and his sister, who appeared to come as part of the package.

'So who's Mr Cholmsey?' was the first thing he said as he strode past her into the house.

Aggie folded her arms and glared resentfully at him as he looked around at his surroundings with the sort of cool contempt she had come to associate with him.

Yes, he was good-looking, all tall and powerful and darkly sexy. But from the very second she had met him, she had been chilled to the bone by his arrogance, his casual contempt for both her and Mark—which he barely bothered to hide—and his thinly veiled threat that he was watching them both and they'd better not overstep the mark.

'Mr Cholmsey's the landlord—and how did you get this address? Why are you here?'

'I had no idea you rented. Stupid me. I was

under the impression that you owned your own house jointly. Now, where did I get that from, I wonder?'

He rested cool, dark eyes on Aggie. 'I was also under the impression that you lived somewhere... slightly less unsavoury. A crashing misconception on my part as well.' However far removed Agatha Collins was from the sort of women Luiz preferred—tall brunettes with legs up to their armpits and amenable, yielding natures—he couldn't deny that she was startlingly pretty. Five-four tops, with pale, curly hair the colour of buttermilk and skin that was satiny smooth. Her eyes were purest aquamarine, offset by dark lashes, as though her creator had been determined to make sure that she stood out from the crowd and had taken one little detail and made it strikingly different.

Aggie flushed and mentally cursed herself for falling in with her brother and Maria. When Luiz had made his first, unwelcome appearance in their lives, she had agreed that she would downplay their financial circumstances, that she would economise harmlessly on the unadorned truth.

'My mum's insisted that Uncle Luiz check

Mark out,' Maria had explained tightly. 'And Uncle Luiz is horribly black-and-white. It'd be better if he thinks that you're…okay… Not exactly rich, but not completely broke either.'

'You still haven't told me what you're doing here,' Aggie dodged.

'Where's your brother?'

'He isn't here and neither is Maria. And when are you going to stop *spying* on us?'

'I'm beginning to think that my *spying* is starting to pay dividends,' Luiz murmured. 'Which one of you told me that you lived in Richmond?' He leaned against the wall and looked down at her with those bottomless dark eyes that always managed to send her nervous system into instant freefall.

'I didn't say that we *lived* in Richmond,' Aggie prevaricated guiltily. 'I probably told you that we go cycling there quite a bit. In the park. It's not my fault that you might have got hold of the wrong end of the stick.'

'I *never* get hold of the wrong end of the stick.' The casual interest which he had seen as an unnecessary chore now blossomed into rampant suspicion. She and her brother had lied about their financial circumstances and had probably persuaded his niece to go along for the ride and back them up. And that, to Luiz, was pointing in only one direction. 'When I got the address of this place, I had to double check because it didn't tally with what I'd been told.' He began removing his coat while Aggie watched in growing dismay.

Every single time she had met Luiz, it had been in one of London's upmarket restaurants. She, Mark and Maria had been treated over time to the finest Italian food money could buy, the best Thai to be found in the country, the most expensive French in the most exclusive area. Pre-warned by Maria that it was her uncle's way of keeping tabs on them, they had been unforthcoming on personal detail and expansive on polite chitchat.

Aggie had bristled at the mere thought that they were being sized up, and she had bristled even more at the nagging suspicion that they had both been found wanting. But restaurants were one thing. Descending on them here was taking it one step too far.

And now his coat was off, which implied that he wasn't about to do the disappearing act she desperately wanted. Something about him unsettled her and here, in this small space, she was even more unsettled.

'Maybe you could get me something to drink,' he inserted smoothly. 'And we can explore what other little lies might come out in the wash while I wait for your brother to show up.'

'Why is it suddenly so important that you talk to Mark?' Aggie asked uneasily. 'I mean, couldn't you have waited? Maybe invited him out for dinner with Maria so that you could try and get to the bottom of his intentions? Again?'

'Things have moved up a gear, regrettably. But I'll come back to that.' He strolled past her through the open door and into the sitting room. The decor here was no more tasteful than it was in the hall. The walls were the colour of off-cheese, depressing despite the old movie posters that had been tacked on. The furniture was an unappealing mix of old and used and tacky, snap-together modern. In one corner, an old television set was propped on a cheap pine unit.

'What do you mean that *things have moved up a gear*?' Aggie demanded as he sat on one of the chairs and looked at her with unhurried thoroughness.

'I guess you know why I've been keeping tabs on your brother.'

'Maria mentioned that her mother can be a little over-protective,' Aggie mumbled. She resigned herself to the fact that Luiz wasn't leaving in a hurry and reluctantly sat down on the chair facing him.

As always, she felt dowdy and underdressed. On the occasions when she had been dragged along to those fancy restaurants—none of which she would ever have sampled had it not been for him—she had rooted out the dressiest clothes in her wardrobe and had still managed to feel cheap and mousey. Now, in baggy, thick jogging bottoms and Mark's jumper, several sizes too big, she felt screamingly, ridiculously frumpy. Which made her resent him even more.

Luiz gave an elegant shrug. 'It pays to be careful. Naturally, when my sister asked me to check your brother out, I tried to talk her out of it.'

'You did?'

'Sure. Maria's a kid and kids have relationships that fall by the wayside. It's life. I was convinced that this relationship would be no different but

I eventually agreed that I would keep an eye on things.'

'By which,' Aggie inserted bitterly, 'you meant that you would quiz us on every aspect of our lives and try and trip us up.'

'Congratulations. You both provided a touchingly united front. I find that I barely know a single personal thing about either of you and it's dawning on me that the few details you've imparted have probably been a tissue of lies—starting with where you live. It would have saved time and effort if I'd employed a detective to ferret out whatever background information was necessary.'

'Maria thought that—'

'Do me a favour. Keep my niece out of this. You live in a dump, which you rent from an unscrupulous landlord. You can barely afford the rent. Tell me, do either of you hold down jobs, or were those fabrications as well?'

'I resent you barging into my house.'

'Mr Cholmsey's house—if you can call it a house.'

'Fine! I still resent you barging in here and insulting me.'

'Tough.'

'In fact, I'm asking you to leave!'

At that, Luiz burst out laughing. 'Do you really think that I've come all the way here so that I can leave the second the questioning gets a little too uncomfortable for you?'

'Well, I don't see the point of you hanging around. Mark and Maria aren't here.'

'I've come because, like I said, things have moved up a gear. It seems that there's now talk of marriage. It's not going to do.'

'Talk of marriage?' Aggie parroted incredulously. 'There's no talk of marriage.'

'At least, none that your brother's told you about. Maybe the touching united front isn't quite as united as you'd like it to be.'

'You…you are just the most *awful* human being I've ever met!'

'I think you've made that glaringly clear on all the occasions that we've met,' Luiz remarked coolly. 'You're entitled to your opinions.'

'So you came here to…what? Warn my brother off? Warn Maria off? They might be young but they're not under age.'

'Maria comes from one of the richest families in Latin America.'

'I beg your pardon?' Aggie looked at him in confusion. Yes, of course she had known that Maria was not the usual hand-to-mouth starving student working the tills on the weekend to help pay for her tuition fees. But *one of the richest families in Latin America?* No wonder she had not been in favour of either of them letting on that they were just normal people struggling to get by on a day-to-day basis!

'You're kidding, right?'

'When it comes to money, I lose my sense of humour.' Luiz abruptly sat forward, elbows resting on his thighs, and looked at her unsmilingly. 'I hadn't planned on taking a hard line, but I'm beginning to do the maths and I don't like the results I'm coming up with.'

Aggie tried and failed to meet his dark, intimidating stare. Why was it that whenever she was in this man's company her usual unflappability was scattered to the four corners? She was reduced to feeling too tight in her skin, too defensive and too self-conscious. Which meant that she could barely think straight.

'I have no idea what you're talking about,' she muttered, staring at her linked fingers while her heart rate sped up and her mouth went dry.

'Wealthy people are often targets,' Luiz gritted, spelling it out in clear syllables just in case she chose to miss the message. 'My niece is extremely wealthy and will be even wealthier when she turns twenty-one. Now it appears that the dalliance I thought would peter out after a couple of months has turned into a marriage proposal.'

'I still can't believe that. You've got your facts wrong.'

'Believe it! And what I'm seeing are a couple of fortune hunters who have lied about their circumstances to try and throw me off course.'

Aggie blanched and stared at him miserably. Those small white fibs had assumed the proportions of mountains. Her brain felt sluggish but already she could see why he would have arrived at the conclusion that he had.

Honest people didn't lie.

'Tell me…is your brother really a musician? Because I've looked him up online and, strangely enough, I can't find him anywhere.'

'Of course he's a musician! He…he plays in a band.'

'And I'm guessing this band hasn't made it big yet…hence his lack of presence on the Internet.'

'Okay! I give up! So we may have…have…'

'Tampered with the truth? Stretched it? Twisted it to the point where it became unrecognisable?'

'Maria said that you're very black-and-white.' Aggie stuck her chin up and met his frowning stare. Now, as had happened before, she marvelled that such sinful physical beauty, the sort of beauty that made people think of putting paint to canvas, could conceal such a cold, ruthless, brutally dispassionate streak.

'Me? Black-and-white?' Luiz was outraged at this preposterous assumption. 'I've never heard anything so ridiculous in my entire life!'

'She said that you form your opinions and you stick to them. You never look outside the box and allow yourself to be persuaded into another direction.'

'That's called strength of character!'

'Well, that's why we weren't inclined to be one hundred percent truthful. Not that we *lied*…

'We just didn't reveal as much as we could have.'

'Such as you live in a rented dump, your brother sings in pubs now and again and you are a teacher—or was that another one of those creative exaggerations?'

'Of course I'm a teacher. I teach primary school. You can check up on me if you like!'

'Well that's now by the by. The fact is, I cannot allow any marriage to take place between my niece and your brother.'

'So you're going to do what, exactly?' Aggie was genuinely bewildered. It was one thing to disapprove of someone else's choices. It was quite another to force them into accepting what you chose to cram down their throat. Luiz, Maria's mother, every single member of their super-wealthy family, for that matter, could rant, storm, wring their hands and deliver threatening lectures—but at the end of the day Maria was her own person and would make up her own mind.

She tactfully decided not to impart that point of view. He claimed that he wasn't black-and-white but she had seen enough evidence of that to convince her that he was. He also had no knowledge whatsoever of how the other half lived. In fact, she doubted that he had ever even come into contact with people who weren't exactly like him, until she and Mark had come along.

'Look.' She relented slightly as another point of view pushed its way through her self-righteous anger. 'I can understand that you might harbour one or two reservations about my brother...'

'Can you?' Luiz asked with biting sarcasm.

Right now he was kicking himself for not having taken a harder look at the pair of them. He was usually as sharp as they came when other people and their motivations were involved. He had had to be. So how had they managed to slip through the net?

Her brother was disingenuous, engaging, apparently open. He looked like the kind of guy who could hold his own with anyone—tall, muscular, with the same shade of blonde hair as his sister but tied back in a ponytail; when he spoke, his voice was low and gentle.

And Agatha—so stunningly pretty that anyone could be forgiven for staring. But, alongside that, she had also been forthright and opinionated. Was that what had taken him in—the combination of two very different personalities? Had they cunningly worked off each other to throw him off-guard? Or had he just failed to take the situation seriously because he hadn't thought the boy's relationship with his niece would ever come to anything? Luisa was famously protective of Maria. Had he just assumed that her request for him to keep an eye out had been more of the same?

At any rate, they had now been caught out in a tangle of lies and that, to his mind, could mean only one thing.

The fact that he'd been a fool for whatever reason was something he would have to live with, but it stuck in his throat.

'And I know how it must look…that we weren't completely open with you. But you have to believe me when I tell you that you have nothing to fear.'

'Point one—fear is an emotion that's alien to me. Point two—I don't have to believe anything you say, which brings me to your question.'

'My question?'

'You wondered what I intended to do about this mess.'

Aggie felt her hackles rise, as they invariably did on the occasions when she had met him, and she made a valiant effort to keep them in check.

'So you intend to warn my brother off,' she said on a sigh.

'Oh, I intend to do much better than that,' Luiz drawled, watching the faint colour in her cheeks and thinking that she was a damn good actress. 'You look as though you could use some money, and I suspect your brother could as well. You have a landlord baying down your neck for unpaid rent.'

'I paid!' Aggie insisted vigorously. 'It's not my fault that there's a postal strike!'

'And whatever you earn as a teacher,' Luiz continued, not bothering to give her protest house room, 'It obviously isn't enough to scrape by. Face it, if you can't afford the rent for a dump like this, then it's pretty obvious that neither of you has a penny to rub together. So my offer to get your brother off the scene and out of my niece's life should put a big smile on your face. In fact, I would go so far as to say that it should make your Christmas.'

'I don't know what you're talking about.'

Those big blue eyes, Luiz thought sourly. They had done a damn good job of throwing him off the scent.

'I'm going to give you and your brother enough money to clear out of this place. You'll each be able to afford to buy somewhere of your own, live the high life, if that's what takes your fancy. And I suspect it probably is...'

'You're going to *pay us off*? To make us *disappear*?'

'Name your price. And naturally your brother can name his. No one has ever accused me of not being a generous man. And on the subject of your brother...when exactly is he due back?' He looked pointedly at his watch and then raised his eyes to her flushed, angry face. She was perched on the very edge of her chair, ramrod-erect, and her knuckles were white where her fingers were biting into the padded seat. She was the very picture of outrage.

'I can't believe I'm hearing this.'

'I'm sure you'll find it remarkably easy to adjust to the thought.'

'You can't just *buy people off*!'

'No? Care to take a small bet on that?' His

eyes were as hard and as cold as the frost gathering outside. 'Doubtless your brother wishes to further his career, if he's even interested in a career. Maybe he'd just like to blow some money on life's little luxuries. Doubtless he ascertained my niece's financial status early on in the relationship and between the two of you you decided that she was your passport to a more lucrative lifestyle. It now appears that he intends to marry her and thereby get his foot through the door, so to speak, but that's not going to happen in a million years. So when you say that I can't *buy people off*? Well, I think you'll find that I can.'

Aggie stared at him open-mouthed. She felt as though she was in the presence of someone from another planet. Was this how the wealthy behaved, as though they owned everything and everyone? As though people were pieces on a chess board to be moved around on a whim and disposed of without scruple? And why was she so surprised when she had always known that he was ruthless, cold-hearted and single-minded?

'Mark and Maria love each other! That must have been obvious to you.'

'I'm sure Maria imagines herself in love. She's

young. She doesn't realise that love is an illusion. And we can sit around chatting all evening, but I still need to know when he'll be here. I want to get this situation sorted as soon as possible.'

'He won't.'

'Come again?'

'I mean,' Aggie ventured weakly, because she knew that the bloodless, heartless man in front of her wasn't going to warm to what she was about to tell him, 'he and Maria decided to have a few days away. A spur-of-the-moment thing. A little pre-Christmas break…'

'Tell me I'm not hearing this.'

'They left yesterday morning.'

She started as he vaulted upright without warning and began pacing the room, his movements restless and menacing.

'Left to go where?' It was a question phrased more like a demand. 'And don't even think of using your looks to pull a fast one.'

'Using my looks?' Aggie felt hot colour crawl into her face. While she had been sitting there in those various restaurants, feeling as awkward and as colourless as a sparrow caught up in a parade of peacocks, had he been looking at her, assessing what she looked like? That thought made her feel weirdly unsteady.

'Where have they gone?' He paused to stand in front of her and Aggie's eyes travelled up—up along that magnificent body sheathed in clothes that looked far too expensive and far too hand-made for their surroundings—until they settled on the forbidding angles of his face. She had never met someone who exuded threat and power the way he did, and who used that to his advantage.

'I don't have to give you that information,' she said stoutly and tried not to quail as his expression darkened.

'I really wouldn't play that game with me if I were you, Agatha.'

'Or else what?'

'Or else I'll make sure that your brother finds himself without a job in the foreseeable future. And the money angle? Off the cards.'

'You can't do that. I mean, you can't do anything to ruin his musical career.'

'Oh no? Please don't put that to the test.'

Aggie hesitated. There was such cool certainty in his voice that she had no doubt that he really would make sure her brother lost his job if she didn't comply and tell him what he wanted.

'Okay. They've gone to a little country hotel in the Lake District,' she imparted reluctantly. 'They wanted a romantic, snowed-in few days, and that part of the world has a lot of sentimental significance for us.' Her bag was on the ground next to her. She reached in, rummaged around and extracted a sheet of paper, confirmation of their booking. 'He gave me this, because it's got all the details in case I wanted to get in touch with him.'

'The Lake District. They've gone to the *Lake District.*' He raked his fingers through his hair, snatched the paper from her and wondered if things could get any worse. The Lake District was not exactly a hop and skip away. Nor was it a plane-ride away. He contemplated the prospect of spending hours behind the wheel of his car in bad driving conditions on a search-and-rescue mission for his sister—because if they were thinking of getting married on the sly, what better time or place? Or else doing battle with the public transport system which was breaking under the weight of the bad weather. He eliminated the public-transport option without hesitation. Which brought him back to the prospect of hours behind the wheel of his car.

'You make it sound as though they've taken a trip to the moon. Well, I guess you'll want to give Maria a call… I'm not sure there's any mobile-phone service there, though. In fact, there isn't. You'll have to phone through to the hotel and get them to transfer you. She can reassure you that they're not about to take a walk down the aisle.' Aggie wondered how her brother was going to deal with Luiz when Luiz waved a wad of notes in front of him and told him to clear off or else. Mark, stupidly, actually liked the man, and stuck up for him whenever Aggie happened to mention how much he got on her nerves.

Not her problem. She struggled to squash her instinctive urge to look out for him. She and Mark had been a tight unit since they were children, when their mother had died and, in the absence of any father, or any relatives for that matter, they had been put into care. Younger by four years, he had been a sickly child, debilitated by frequent asthma attacks. Like a surrogate mother hen, she had learnt to take care of him and to put his needs ahead of her own. She had gained strength, allowing him the freedom to be the gentle, dreamy child who had matured into a gentle, dreamy adult—despite his long hair, his earring and the tattoo on his shoulder which seemed to announce a different kind of person.

'Well, now that you know where they are, I guess you'll be leaving.'

Luiz, looking at her down-bent head, pondered this sequence of events. Missing niece. Missing boyfriend. Long trip to locate them.

'I don't know why I didn't see this coming,' he mused. 'Having a few days away would be the perfect opportunity for your brother to seal the deal. Maybe my presence on the scene alerted him to the fact that time wouldn't be on his side when it came to marrying my niece. Maybe he figured that the courtship would have to be curtailed and the main event brought forward...a winter wedding. Very romantic.'

'That's the most ridiculous thing I've ever heard!'

'I'd be surprised if you didn't say that. Well, it's not going to happen. We'll just have to make sure that we get to that romantic hideaway and surprise them before they have time to do anything regrettable.'

'*We?*'

Luiz looked at her with raised eyebrows. 'Well, you don't imagine that I'm going to go there on my own and leave you behind so that you can get on the phone and warn your brother of my impending arrival, do you?'

'You're crazy! I'm not going anywhere with you, Luiz Montes!'

'It's not ideal timing, and I can't say that I haven't got better things to do on a Friday evening, but I can't see a way out of it. I anticipate we'll be there by tomorrow lunchtime, so you'll have to pack enough for a weekend and make it quick. I'll need to get back to my place so that I can throw some things in a bag.'

'You're not hearing what I'm saying!'

'Correction. I am hearing. I'm just choosing to ignore what you're saying because none of it will make any difference to what I intend to do.'

'I refuse to go along with this!'

'Here's the choice. We go, I chat to your brother, I dangle my financial inducement in front of him... A few tears all round to start with but in the end everyone's happy. Plan B is I send my men up to physically bring him back to London, where he'll find that life can be very uncomfortable when all avenues of work are dried up. I'll put the word out in the music industry that he's not to be touched with a barge pole. You'd be surprised if you knew the extent of my connections. One word—*vast*. I'm guessing that as his loyal, devoted sister, option two might be tough to swallow.'

'You are…are…'

'Yes, yes, yes. I know what you think of me. I'll give you ten minutes to be at the front door. If you're not there, I'm coming in to get you. And look on the bright side, Agatha. I'm not even asking you to take time off from your job. You'll be delivered safely back here by Monday morning, in one piece and with a bank account that's stuffed to the rafters. And we'll never have to lay eyes on each other again!'

CHAPTER TWO

'I just can't believe that you would blackmail me into this,' was the first thing she said as she joined him at the front door, bag reluctantly in hand.

'Blackmail? I prefer to call it *persuasion*.' Luiz pushed himself off the wall against which he had been lounging, calculating how much work he would be missing and also working out that his date for the following night wasn't going to be overjoyed at this sudden road trip. Not that that unduly bothered him. In fact, to call it a *date* was wildly inappropriate. He had had four dates with Chloe Bern and on the fifth he had broken it gently to her that things between them weren't working out. She hadn't taken it well. This was the sixth time he would be seeing her and it would be to repeat what he had already told her on date five.

Aggie snorted derisively. She had feverishly

tried to find a way of backing out, but all exits seemed to have been barred. Luiz was in hunting mode and she knew that the threats he had made hadn't been empty ones. For the sake of her brother, she had no choice but to agree to this trip and she felt like exploding with anger.

Outside, the weather was grimly uninviting, freezing cold and with an ominous stillness in the atmosphere.

She followed him to his fancy car, incongruous between the battered, old run-arounds on either side, and made another inarticulate noise as he beeped it open.

'You're going to tell me,' Luiz said, settling into the driver's seat and waiting for her as she strapped herself in, 'that this is a pointless toy belonging to someone with more money than sense. Am I right?'

'You must be a mind reader,' Aggie said acidly.

'Not a mind reader. Just astute when it comes to remembering conversations we've had in the past.' He started the engine and the sports car purred to life.

'You can't have remembered everything I've said to you,' Aggie muttered uncomfortably.

'Everything. How do you think I'm so sure that you never mentioned renting this dump here?' He threw her a sidelong glance. 'I'm thinking that your brother doesn't contribute greatly to the family finances?' Which in turn made him wonder who would be footing the bill for the romantic getaway. If Aggie barely earned enough to keep the roof over her head, then it stood to reason that Mark earned even less, singing songs in a pub. His jaw tightened at the certainty that Maria was already the goose laying the golden eggs.

'He can't,' Aggie admitted reluctantly. 'Not that I mind, because I don't.'

'That's big of you. Most people would resent having to take care of their kid brother when he's capable of taking care of himself.' They had both been sketchy on the details of Mark's job and Luiz, impatient with a task that had been foisted onto his shoulders, had not delved deeply enough. He had been content enough to ascertain that his niece wasn't going out with a potential axe-murderer, junkie or criminal on the run. 'So…he works in a bar and plays now and then in a band. You might as well tell me the truth,

Agatha. Considering there's no longer any point in keeping secrets.'

Aggie shrugged. 'Yes, he works in a bar and gets a gig once every few weeks. But his talent is really with songwriting. You'll probably think that I'm spinning you a fairy story, because you're suspicious of everything I say...'

'With good reason, as it turns out.'

'But he's pretty amazing at composing. Often in the evenings, while I'm reading or else going through some of the homework from the kids or preparing for classes, he'll sit on the sofa playing his guitar and working on his latest song over and over until he thinks he's got it just right.'

'And you never thought to mention that to me because...?'

'I'm sure Mark told you that he enjoyed songwriting.'

'He told me that he was a musician. He may have mentioned that he knew people in the entertainment business. The general impression was that he was an established musician with an established career. I don't believe I ever heard you contradict him.'

The guy was charming but broke, and his

state of penury was no passing inconvenience. He was broke because he lived in a dreamworld of strumming guitars and dabbling about with music sheets.

Thinking about it now, Luiz could see why Maria had fallen for the guy. She was the product of a fabulously wealthy background. The boys she had met had always had plentiful supplies of money. Many of them either worked in family businesses or were destined to. A musician, with a notebook and a guitar slung over his shoulder, rustling up cocktails in a bar by night? On every level he had been her accident waiting to happen. No wonder they had all seen fit to play around with the truth! Maria was sharp enough to have known that a whiff of the truth would have had alarm bells ringing in his head.

'I happen to be very proud of my brother,' Aggie said stiffly. 'It's important that people find their own way. I know you probably don't have much time for that.'

'I have a lot of time for that, provided it doesn't impact my family.'

The traffic was horrendous but eventually they cleared it and, after a series of back roads, emerged at a square of elegant red-bricked Victorian houses in the centre of which was a gated, private park.

There had been meals out but neither she nor her brother had ever actually been asked over to Luiz's house.

This was evidence of wealth on a shocking scale. Aside from Maria's expensive bags, which she'd laughingly claimed she couldn't resist and could afford because her family was 'not badly off', there had been nothing to suggest that not badly off had actually meant staggeringly rich.

Even though the restaurants had been grand and expensive, Aggie had never envisioned the actual lifestyle that Luiz enjoyed to accompany them. She had no passing acquaintance with money. Lifestyles of the rich and famous were things she occasionally read about in magazines and dismissed without giving it much thought. Getting out of the car, she realised that, between her and her brother and Luiz and his family, there was a chasm so vast that the thought of even daring to cross it gave her a headache.

Once again she was reluctantly forced to see

why Maria's mother had asked Luiz to watch the situation.

Once again she backtracked over their glossing over of their circumstances and understood why Luiz was now reacting the way he was. He was so wrong about them both but he was trapped in his own circumstances and had probably been weaned on suspicion from a very young age.

'Are you going to come out?' Luiz bent down to peer at her through the open car door. 'Or are you going to stay there all night gawping?'

'I wasn't gawping!' Aggie slammed the car door behind her and followed him into a house, a four-storey house that took her breath away, from the pale marble flooring to the dramatic paintings on the walls to the sweeping banister that led up to yet more impeccable elegance.

He strode into a room to the right and after a few seconds of dithering Aggie followed him inside. He hadn't glanced at her once. Just shed his coat and headed straight for his answer machine, which he flicked on while loosening his tie.

She took the opportunity to look round her: stately proportions and the same pale marbled flooring, with softly faded silk rugs to break the expanse. The furniture was light leather and the floor-to-ceiling curtains thick velvet, a shade deeper in colour than the light pinks of the rugs.

She was vaguely aware that he was listening to what seemed to be an interminable series of business calls, until the last message, when the breathy voice of a woman reminded him that she would be seeing him tomorrow and that she couldn't wait.

At that, Aggie's ears pricked up. He might very well have accused her of being shady when it came to her and her brother's private lives. She now realised that she actually knew precious little about *him*.

He wasn't married; that much she knew for sure because Maria had confided that the whole family was waiting for him to tie the knot and settle down. Beyond that, of course, he *would* have a girlfriend. No one as eligible as Luiz Montes would be without one. She looked at him surreptitiously and wondered what the owner of that breathy, sexy voice looked like.

'I'm going to have a quick shower. I'll be back down in ten minutes and then we'll get going. No point hanging around.'

Aggie snapped back to the present. She was blushing. She could feel it. Blushing as she speculated on his private life.

'Make yourself at home,' Luiz told her drily. 'Feel free to explore.'

'I'm fine here, thank you very much.' She perched awkwardly on the edge of one of the pristine leather sofas and rested her hands primly on her lap.

'Suit yourself.'

But as soon as he had left the room, she began exploring like a kid in a toyshop, touching some of the clearly priceless *objets d'art* he had randomly scattered around: a beautiful bronze figurine of two cheetahs on the long, low sideboard against the wall; a pair of vases that looked very much like the real thing from a Chinese dynasty; she gazed at the abstract on the wall and tried to decipher the signature.

'Do you like what you see?' Luiz asked from behind her and she started and went bright red.

'I've never been in a place like this before,' Aggie said defensively.

Her mouth went dry as she looked at him. He was dressed in a pair of black jeans and a grey-

and-black-striped woollen jumper. She could see the collar of his shirt underneath, soft grey flannel. All the other times she had seen him he had been formally dressed, almost as though he had left work to meet them at whatever mega-expensive restaurant he had booked. But this was casual and he was really and truly drop-dead sexy.

'It's a house, not a museum. Shall we go?' He flicked off the light as she left the sitting room and pulled out his mobile phone to instruct his driver to bring the four-by-four round.

'*My* house is a house.' Aggie was momentarily distracted from her anger at his accusations as she stared back at the mansion behind her and waited with him for the car to be delivered.

'Correction. Your house is a hovel. Your landlord deserves to be shot for charging a tenant for a place like that. You probably haven't noticed, but in the brief time I was there I spotted the kind of cracks that advertise a problem with damp—plaster falling from the walls and patches on the ceiling that probably mean you'll have a leak sooner rather than later.'

The four-by-four, shiny and black, slowed and Luiz's driver got out.

'There's nothing I can do about that,' Aggie huffed, climbing into the passenger seat. 'Anyway, you live in a different world to me…to us. It's almost impossible to find somewhere cheap to rent in London.'

'There's a difference between cheap and hazardous. Just think of what you could buy if you had the money in your bank account…' He manoeuvred the big car away from the kerb. 'Nice house in a smart postcode… Quaint little garden at the back… You like gardening, don't you? I believe it's one of those things you mentioned… although it's open to debate whether you were telling the truth or lying to give the right impression.'

'I wasn't lying! I love gardening.'

'London gardens are generally small but you'd be surprised to discover what you can get for the right price.'

'I would never accept a penny from you, Luiz Montes!'

'You don't mean that.'

That tone of comfortable disbelief enraged her. 'I'm not interested in money!' She turned to him, looked at his aristocratic dark profile, and felt that familiar giddy feeling.

'Call me cynical, but I have yet to meet someone who isn't interested in money. They might make noises about money not being able to buy happiness and the good things in life being free, but they like the things money can do and the freebies go through the window when more expensive ways of being happy enter the equation. Tell me seriously that you didn't enjoy those meals you had out.'

'Yes, I *enjoyed* them, but I wouldn't miss them if they weren't there.'

'And what about your brother? Is he as noble minded as you?'

'Neither of us are materialistic, if that's what you mean. You met him. Did he strike you as the sort of person who…who would lead Maria on because of what he thought he could get out of her? I mean, didn't you like him at all?'

'I liked him, but that's not the point.'

'You mean the point is that Maria can go out with someone from a different background, just so long as there's no danger of getting serious, because the only person she would be allowed to settle down with would be someone of the same social standing as her.'

'You say that as though there's something wrong with it.'

'I don't want to talk about this. It's not going to get us anywhere.' She fell silent and watched the slow-moving traffic around her, a sea of headlights illuminating late-night shoppers, people hurrying towards the tube or to catch a bus. At this rate, it would be midnight before they cleared London.

'Would you tell me something?' she asked to break the silence.

'I'm listening.'

'Why didn't you try and put an end to their relationship from the start? I mean, why did you bother taking us out for all those meals?'

'Not my place to interfere. Not at that point, at any rate. I'd been asked to keep an eye on things, to meet your brother and, as it turns out, you too, because the two of you seem to be joined at the hip.' He didn't add that, having not had very much to do with his niece in the past, he had found that he rather enjoyed their company. He had liked listening to Mark and Maria entertain him with their chat about movies and music. And even more he had liked the way Aggie had argued with him, had liked the way it had challenged him into making an effort to get her to laugh. It had all made a change from the extravagant social events to which he was invited, usually in a bid by a company to impress him.

'We're not joined at the hip! We're close because...' Because of their background of foster care, but that was definitely something they had kept to themselves.

'Because you lost your parents?'

'That's right.' She had told him in passing, almost the first time she had met him, that their parents were dead and had swiftly changed the subject. Just another muddled half-truth that would further make him suspicious of their motives.

'Apart from which, I thought that my sister had been overreacting to the whole thing. Maria is an only child without a father. Luisa is prone to pointless worrying.'

'I can't imagine you taking orders from your sister.'

'You haven't met Luisa or any of my five sisters. If you had, you wouldn't make that observation.' He laughed and Aggie felt the breath catch in her throat because, for once, his laughter stemmed from genuine amusement.

'What are they like?'

'All older than me and all bossy.' He grinned sideways at her. 'It's easier to surrender than to cross them. In a family of six women, my father and I know better than to try and argue. It would be easier staging a land war in Asia.'

That glimpse of his humanity unsettled Aggie. But she had had glimpses of it before, she recalled uneasily. Times when he had managed to make her forget how dislikeable he was, when he had recounted something with such dry wit that she had caught herself trying hard to stifle a laugh. He might be hateful, judgemental and unfair, he might represent a lot of things she disliked, but there was no denying that he was one of the most intelligent men she had ever met— and, when it suited him, one of the most entertaining. She had contrived to forget all of that but, stuck here with him, it was coming back to her fast and she had to fumble her way out of her momentary distraction.

'I couldn't help overhearing those messages earlier on at the house,' she said politely.

'Messages? What are you talking about?'

'Lots of business calls. I guess you're having to sacrifice working time for this...unless you don't work on a weekend.'

'If you're thinking of using a few messages you overheard as a way of trying to talk me out of this trip, then you can forget it.'

'I wasn't thinking of doing that. I was just being polite.'

'In that case, you can rest assured that there's nothing that can't wait until Monday when I'm back in London. I have my mobile and if anything urgent comes up, then I can deal with it on the move. Nice try, though.'

'What about that other message? I gather you'll be missing a date with someone tomorrow night?'

Luiz stiffened. 'Again, nothing that can't be handled.'

'Because I would feel very guilty otherwise.'

'Don't concern yourself with my private life, Aggie.'

'Why not?' Aggie risked. 'You're concerning yourself with mine.'

'Slightly different scenario, wouldn't you agree? To the best of my knowledge, I haven't been caught trying to con anyone recently. My private life isn't the one under the spotlight.'

'You're impossible! You're so...*blinkered*! Did you know that Maria was the one who pursued Mark?'

'Do me a favour.'

'She was,' Aggie persisted. 'Mark was playing at one of the pubs and she and her friends went to hear them. She went to meet him after the gig and she gave him her mobile number, told him to get in touch.'

'I'm finding that hard to believe, but let's suppose you're telling the truth. I don't see what that has to do with anything. Whether she chased your brother or your brother chased her, the end result is the same. An heiress is an extremely lucrative proposition for someone in his position.' He switched on the radio and turned it to the traffic news.

London was crawling. The weather forecasters had been making a big deal of snow to come. There was nothing at the moment but people were still rushing to get back home and the roads were gridlocked.

Aggie wearily closed her eyes and leaned back. She was hungry and exhausted and trying to get through to Luiz was like beating her head against a brick wall.

She came to suddenly to the sound of Luiz's low, urgent voice and she blinked herself out of sleep. She had no idea how long she had been dozing, or even how she could manage to doze at all when her thoughts were all over the place.

He was on his phone, and from the sounds of it not enjoying the conversation he was having.

In fact, sitting up and stifling a yawn, it dawned on her that the voice on the other end of the mobile was the same smoky voice that had left a message on his answer machine earlier on, and the reason Aggie knew that was because the smoky voice had become high-pitched and shrill. Not only could *she* hear every word the other woman was saying, she guessed that if she rolled down her window the people in the car behind them would be able to as well.

'This is not the right time for this conversation...' Luiz was saying in a harried, urgent voice.

'Don't you dare hang up on me! I'll just keep calling! I deserve better than this!'

'Which is why you should be thanking me for putting an end to our relationship, Chloe. You do deserve a hell of a lot better than me.'

Aggie rolled her eyes. Wasn't that the oldest trick in the book? The one men used when they wanted to exit a relationship with their consciences intact? Take the blame for everything, manage to convince their hapless girlfriend that breaking up is all for her own good and then walk away feeling as though they've done their good deed for the day.

She listened while Luiz, obviously resigning himself to a conversation he hadn't initiated and didn't want, explained in various ways why they weren't working as a couple.

She had never seen him other than calm, self-assured, in complete control of himself and everything around him. People jumped to attention when he spoke and he had always had that air of command that was afforded to people of influence and power.

He was not that man when he finally ended the

call to the sound of virulent abuse on the other end of the line.

'Well?' he demanded grittily. 'I am sure you have an opinion on the conversation you unfortunately had to overhear.'

When she had asked him about his private life, this was not what she had been expecting. He had quizzed her about hers, about her brother's; a little retaliation had seemed only fair. But that conversation had been intensely personal.

'You've broken up with someone and I'm sorry about that,' Aggie said quietly. 'I know that it's wretched when a relationship comes to an end, especially if you've invested in it, and of course I don't want to talk about that. It's your business.'

'I like that.'

'What?'

'Your kind words of sympathy. Believe me when I tell you that there's nothing that could have snapped me out of my mood as efficiently as that.'

'What are you talking about?' Aggie asked, confused. She looked at him to see him smiling with amusement and when he flicked her a sideways glance his smile broadened.

'I'm not dying of a broken heart,' he assured her. 'In fact, if you'd been listening, I'm the one who instigated the break-up.'

'Yes,' Aggie agreed smartly. 'Which doesn't mean that it didn't hurt.'

'Are you speaking from experience?'

'Well, yes, as a matter of fact!'

'I'm inclined to believe you,' Luiz drawled. 'So why did you dump him? Wasn't he man enough to deal with your wilful, argumentative nature?'

'I'm neither of those things!' Aggie reddened and glared at his averted profile.

'On that point, we're going to have to differ.'

'I'm only argumentative with *you*, Luiz Montes! And perhaps that's because you've accused me of being a liar and an opportunist, plotting with my brother to take advantage of your niece!'

'Give it a rest. You have done nothing but argue with me since the second you met me. You've made telling comments about every restaurant, about the value of money, about people who think they can rule the world from a chequebook... You've covered all the ground when it comes to letting me know that you disapprove of wealth. Course, how was I to know that those were just cleverly positioned comments to downplay what you were all about? But let's leave that aside for the moment. Why did you dump the poor guy?'

'If you must know,' Aggie said, partly because constant arguing was tiring and partly because she wanted to let him know that Stu had not found her in the least bit argumentative, 'he became too jealous and too possessive, and I don't like those traits.'

'Amazing. I think we've discovered common ground.'

'Meaning?'

'Chloe went from obliging to demanding in record time.' They had finally cleared London and Luiz realised that unless they continued driving through the night they would have to take a break at some point along the route. It was also beginning to snow. For the moment, though, that was something he would keep to himself.

'Never a good trait as far as I am concerned.' He glanced at Aggie and was struck again by the extreme ultra-femininity of her looks. He imagined that guys could get sucked in by those looks only to discover a wildcat behind the angelic front. Whatever scam she and her brother had concocted between them, she had definitely been the brains behind it. Hell, he could almost appreciate the sharp, outspoken intelligence there. Under the low-level sniping, she was a woman a guy could have a conversation with and that, Luiz conceded, was something. He didn't have much use for conversation with women, not when there were always so many more entertaining ways of spending time with them.

Generally speaking, the women he had gone out with had never sparked curiosity. Why would they? They had always been a known quantity, wealthy socialites with impeccable pedigrees. He was thirty-three years old and could honestly say that he had never deviated from the expected.

With work always centre-stage, it had been very easy to slide in and out of relationships with women who were socially acceptable. In a world where greed and avarice lurked around every corner, it made sense to eliminate the opportunist by making sure never to date anyone who could fall into that category. He had never questioned it. If none of the women in his past had ever succeeded in capturing his attention for longer than ten seconds, then he wasn't bothered.

His sisters, bar two, had all done their duty and reproduced, leaving him free to live his life the way he saw fit.

'So...what do you mean? That the minute a woman wants something committed you back away? Was that what your ex-girlfriend was guilty of?'

'I make it my duty never to make promises I can't keep,' Luiz informed her coolly. 'I'm always straight with women. I'm not in it for the long run. Chloe, unfortunately, began thinking that the rules of the game could be changed somewhere along the line. I should have seen the signs, of course,' he continued half to himself. 'The minute a woman starts making noises about wanting to spend a night in and play happy families is the minute the warning bells should start going off.'

'And they didn't?' Aggie was thinking that wanting to spend the odd night in didn't sound like an impossible dream or an undercover marriage proposal.

'She *was* very beautiful,' Luiz conceded with a laugh.

'Was that why you went out with her? Because of the way she looked?'

'I'm a great believer in the power of sexual attraction.'

'That's very shallow.'

Luiz laughed again and slanted an amused look at her. 'You're not into sex?'

Aggie reddened and her heart started pounding like a drum beat inside her. 'That's none of your business!'

'Some women aren't.' Luiz pushed the boundaries. Unlike the other times he had seen her, he now had her all to himself, undiluted by the presence of Mark and his niece. Naturally he would use the time to find out everything he could about her and her brother, all the better to prepare him for when they finally made it to the Lake District. But for now it was no hardship trying to prise underneath her prickly exterior to find out what made her tick. They were cooped up together in a car. What else was there to do? 'Are you one of those women?' he asked silkily.

'I happen to think that sex isn't the most important thing in a relationship!'

'That's probably because you haven't experienced good sex.'

'That's the most ridiculous thing I've ever heard

in my life!' But her face was hot and flushed and she was finding it difficult to breathe properly.

'I hope I'm not embarrassing you…'

'I'm not *embarrassed*. I just think that this is an inappropriate conversation.'

'Because…?'

'Because I don't want to be here. Because you're dragging me off on a trek to find my brother so that you can accuse him of being an opportunist and fling money at him so that he goes away. Because you think that we can be bought off.'

'That aside…' He switched on his wipers as the first flurries of snow began to cloud the glass. 'We're here and we can't maintain hostilities indefinitely. And I hate to break this to you, but it looks as though our trip might end up taking a little longer than originally anticipated.'

'What do you mean?'

'Look ahead of you. The traffic is crawling and the snow's started to fall. I can keep driving for another hour or so but then we're probably going to have to pull in somewhere for the night. In fact, keep your eyes open. I'm going to divert to the nearest town and we're going to find somewhere overnight.'

CHAPTER THREE

IN THE end, she had to look up somewhere on his phone because they appeared to have entered hotel-free territory.

'It's just one reason why I try to never leave London,' Luiz muttered in frustration. 'Wide, empty open spaces with nothing inside them. Not even a halfway decent hotel, from the looks of it.'

'That's what most people love about getting out of London.'

'Repeat—different strokes for different folks. What have you found?' They had left the grinding traffic behind them. Now he had to contend with dangerously icy roads and thickly falling snow that limited his vision. He glanced across but couldn't see her face because of the fall of soft, finely spun golden hair across it.

'You're going to be disappointed because there are no fancy hotels, although there *is* a B and B about five miles away and it's rated very highly.

It's a bit of a detour but it's the only thing I've been able to locate.'

'Address.' He punched it into his guidance system and relaxed at the thought that he would be able to take a break. 'Read me what it says about this place.'

'I don't suppose anyone's ever told you this but you talk to people as though they're your servants. You just expect people to do what you want them to do without question.'

'I would be inclined to agree with that,' Luiz drawled. 'But for the fact that you don't slot into that category, so there goes your argument. I ask you to simply tell me about this bed and breakfast, which you'll do but not until you let me know that you resent the request, and you resent the request for no other reason that I happen to be the one making it. The down side of accusing someone of being black-and-white is that you should be very sure that you don't fall into the same category yourself.'

Aggie flushed and scowled. 'Five bedrooms, two *en suite*, a sitting room. And the price includes a full English breakfast. There's also a charming garden area but I don't suppose that's relevant considering the weather. And I'm the least prejudiced person I know. I'm extremely open minded!'

'Five bedrooms. Two *en suite*. Is there nothing a little less basic in the vicinity?'

'We're in the country now,' Aggie informed him tersely, half-annoyed because he hadn't taken her up on what she had said. 'There are no five-star hotels, if that's what you mean.'

'You know,' Luiz murmured softly, straining to see his way forward when the wipers could barely handle the fall of snow on the windscreen, 'I can understand your hostility towards me, but what I find a little more difficult to understand is your hostility towards all displays of wealth. The first time I met you, you made it clear that expensive restaurants were a waste of money when all over the world people were going without food... But hell, I don't want to get into this. It's hard enough trying to concentrate on not going off the road without launching into yet another pointless exchange of words. You're going to have to look out for a sign.'

Of course, he had no interest in her personally, not beyond wanting to protect his family and their wealth from her, so she should be able to disregard everything he said. But he had still managed to make her feel like a hypocrite and Aggie shifted uncomfortably.

'I'm sorry I can't offer to share the driving,' she muttered, to smooth over her sudden confusion at the way he had managed to turn her notions about herself on their head. 'But I don't have my driving licence.'

'I wouldn't ask you to drive even if you did,' Luiz informed her.

'Because women need protecting?' But she was half-smiling when she said that.

'Because I would have a nervous breakdown.'

Aggie stifled a giggle. He had a talent for making her want to laugh when she knew she should be on the defensive. 'That's very chauvinistic.'

'I think you've got the measure of me. I don't make a good back-seat driver.'

'That's probably because you feel that you always have to be in control,' Aggie pointed out. 'And I suppose you really are always in control, aren't you?'

'I like to be.' Luiz had slowed the car right down. Even though it was a powerful four-wheel drive, he knew that the road was treacherous and ungritted. 'Are you going to waste a few minutes trying to analyse me now?'

'I wouldn't dream of it!' But she was feverishly analysing him in her head, eaten up with curiosity as to what made this complex man tick. She didn't care, of course. It was a game generated by the fact that they were in close proximity, but she caught herself wondering whether his need for absolute control wasn't an inherited obligation. He was an only son of a Latin American magnate. Had he been trained to see himself as ruler of all he surveyed? It occurred to her that this wasn't the first time she had found herself wondering about him, and that was an uneasy thought.

'Anyway, we're here.' They were now in a village and she could see that it barely encompassed a handful of shops, in between and around which radiated small houses, the sort of houses found in books depicting the perfect English country village. The bed and breakfast was a tiny semi-detached house, very easily bypassed were it not for the sign swinging outside, barely visible under the snow.

It was very late and the roads were completely deserted. Even the bed and breakfast was plunged in darkness, except for two outside lights which just about managed to illuminate the front of the house and a metre or two of garden in front.

With barely contained resignation, Luiz pulled up outside and killed the engine.

'It looks wonderful,' Aggie breathed, taken with the creamy yellow stone and the perfectly proportioned leaded windows. She could picture the riot of colour in summer with all manner of flowers ablaze in the front garden and the soporific sound of the bees buzzing between them.

'Sorry?' Luiz wondered whether they were looking at the same house.

' 'Course, I would rather not be here with *you*,' Aggie emphasised. 'But it's beautiful. Especially with the snow on the ground and on the roof. Gosh, it's really deep as well! That's the one thing I really miss about living in the south. Snow.'

On that tantalising statement, she flung open the car door and stepped outside, holding her arms out wide and her head tilted up so that the snow could fall directly onto her face.

In the act of reaching behind him to extract

their cases, Luiz paused to stare at her. She had pulled some fingerless gloves out of her coat pocket and stuck them on and standing like that, arms outstretched, she looked young, vulnerable and achingly innocent, a child reacting to the thrill of being out in the snow.

Beside the point what she looks like, he told himself, breaking the momentary spell to get their bags. She was pretty. He knew that. He had known that from the very first second he had set eyes on her. The world was full of pretty women, especially *his* world, which was not only full of pretty women but pretty women willing to throw themselves at him.

Aggie began walking towards the house, her feet sinking into the snow, and only turned to look around when he had slammed shut the car door and was standing in front of it, a bag in either hand—his mega-expensive bag, her forlorn and cheaply made one which had been her companion from the age of fourteen when she had spent her first night at a friend's house.

He looked just so incongruous. She couldn't see his expression because it was dark but she imagined that he would be bewildered, removed from his precious creature comforts and thrown into a world far removed from the expensive one he occupied. A bed and breakfast with just five bedrooms, only two of which were *en suite*! What a horror story for him! Not to mention the fact that he would have to force himself to carry on being polite to the sister of an unscrupulous opportunist who was plotting to milk his niece for her millions. He was lead actor in the middle of his very worst nightmare and as he stood there, watching her, she reached down to scoop up a handful of snow, cold and crisp and begging to be moulded into a ball.

All her anger and frustration towards him and towards herself for reacting to him when she should be able to be cool and dismissive went into that throw, and she held her breath as the snowball arched upwards and travelled with deadly accuracy towards him, hitting him right in the middle of that broad, muscled, arrogant chest.

She didn't know who was more surprised. Her, for having thrown it in the first place, or him for being hit for the first time in his life by a snowball. Before he could react, she turned her back and began plodding to the front door.

He deserved that, she told herself nervously. He was insulting, offensive and dismissive. He had accused her and her brother in the worst possible way of the worst possible things and had not been prepared to nurture any doubts that he might be wrong. Plus he had had the cheek to make her question herself when she hadn't done anything wrong!

Nevertheless, she didn't want to look back over her shoulder for fear of seeing what his reaction might be at her small act of resentful rebellion.

'Nice shot!' she heard him shout, at which she began to turn around when she felt the cold, wet compacted blow of his retaliation. She had launched her missile at his chest and he had done the same, and his shot was even more faultless than hers had been.

Aggie's mouth dropped open and she looked at him incredulously as he began walking towards her.

'Good shot. Bull's eye.' He grinned at her and he was transformed, the harsh, unforgiving lines of his face replaced by a sex appeal that was so powerful that it almost knocked her sideways. The breath caught in her throat and she found that she was staring up at him while her thoughts tumbled around as though they had been tossed into a spin drier turned to full speed.

'You too,' was all she could think of saying. 'Where did you learn to throw a snowball?'

'Boarding school. Captain of the cricket team. I was their fast bowler.' He rang the doorbell but he didn't take his eyes from her face. 'Did you think that I was so pampered that I wouldn't have been able to retaliate?' he taunted softly.

'Yes.' Her mouth felt as though it was stuffed with cotton wool. Pampered? Yes, of course he was…and yet a less pampered man it would have been hard to find. How did that make sense?

'Where did *you* learn to throw a shot like that? You hit me from thirty metres away. Through thick snow and poor visibility.'

Aggie blinked in an attempt to gather her scattered wits, but she still heard herself say, with complete honesty, 'We grew up with snow in winter. We learned to build snowmen and have snowball fights and there were always lots of kids around because we were raised in a children's home.'

Deafening silence greeted this remark. She

hadn't planned on saying that, but out it had come, and she could have kicked herself. Thankfully she was spared the agony of his contempt by the door being pulled open and they were ushered inside by a short, jolly woman in her sixties who beamed at them as though they were much expected long-lost friends, even though it was nearly ten and she had probably been sound asleep.

Of course there was room for them! Business was never good in winter...just the one room let to a long-standing resident who worked nearby during the week...not that there was any likelihood that he would be leaving for his home in Yorkshire at the weekend...not in this snow... had they seen anything like it...?

The jovial patter kept Aggie's turbulent thoughts temporarily at bay. Regrettably, one of the *en suite* rooms was occupied by the long-standing resident who wouldn't be able to return to Yorkshire at the weekend. As she looked brightly between them to see who would opt for the remaining *en suite* bedroom, Aggie smiled innocently at Luiz until he was forced to do the expected and concede to sharing a bathroom.

She could feel him simmering next to her as they were proudly shown the sitting room, where there was 'a wide assortment of channels on the telly because they had recently had cable fitted'. And the small breakfast room where they could have the best breakfast in the village, and also dinner if they would like, although because of the hour she could only run to sandwiches just now...

Aggie branched off into her own, generously proportioned and charming bedroom and nodded blandly when Luiz informed her that he would see her in the sitting room in ten minutes. They both needed something to eat.

There was just time to wash her face, no time at all to unpack or have a bath and get into fresh clothes. Downstairs, Luiz was waiting for her. She heard the rumble of his voice and low laughter as he talked to the landlady. Getting closer, she could make out that he was explaining that they were on their way to visit relatives, that the snow had temporarily cut short their journey. That, yes, public transport would have been more sensible but for the fact that the trains had responded to the bad weather by going on strike. However, what a blessing in disguise, because how else would they have discovered this charming part of the world? And perhaps she could bring them a bottle of wine with their sandwiches...whatever she had to hand would do as long as it was cold...

'So...' Luiz drawled as soon as they had the sitting room to themselves. 'The truth is now all coming out in the wash. Were you ever going to tell me about your background or were you intending to keep that little titbit to yourself until it no longer mattered who knew?'

'I didn't think it was relevant.'

'Do me a favour, Aggie.'

'I'm not ashamed of...' She sighed and ran her fingers through her hair. It was cosy in here and beautifully warm, with an open fire at one end. He had removed his jumper and rolled his sleeves up and her eyes strayed to his arms, sprinkled with dark hair. He had an athlete's body and she had to curb the itch to stare at him. She didn't know where that urge was coming from. Or had it been there from the start?

Wine was brought to them and she felt like she needed some. One really big glass to help her through this conversation...

'You're not ashamed of...? Concealing the truth?'

'I didn't think of it as concealing the truth.'

'Well, forgive me, but it seems a glaring omission.'

'It's not something I talk about.'

'Why not?'

'Why do you think?' She glared at him, realised that the big glass of wine had somehow disappeared in record time and didn't refuse when her wine glass was topped up.

Luiz flushed darkly. It wouldn't do to forget that this was not a date. He wasn't politely delving down conversational avenues as a prelude to sex. Omissions like this mattered, given the circumstances. But those huge blue eyes staring at him with a mixture of uncertainty and accusation were getting to him.

'You tell me.'

'People can be judgemental,' Aggie muttered defensively. 'As soon as you say that you grew up in a children's home, people switch off. You wouldn't understand. How could you? You've always led the kind of life people like us dreamt about. A life of luxury, with family all around you. Even if your sisters were bossy and told you what to do when you were growing up. It's a different world.'

'I'm not without imagination,' Luiz said gruffly.

'But this is just something else that you can hold against us...just another nail in the coffin.'

Yes, it was! But he was still curious to find out about that shady background she had kept to herself. He barely noticed when a platter of sandwiches was placed in front of them, accompanied by an enormous salad, along with another bottle of excellent wine.

'You went to a boarding school. I went to the local comprehensive where people sniggered because I was one of those kids from a children's home. Sports days were a nightmare. Everyone else would have their family there, shouting and yelling them on. I just ran and ran and ran and pretended that there were people there cheering *me* on. Sometimes Gordon or Betsy—the couple who ran the home—would try and come but it was difficult. I could deal with all of that but Mark was always a lot more sensitive.'

'Which is why you're so close now. You said that your parents were dead.'

'They are.' She helped herself to a bit more wine, even though she was unaccustomed to alcohol and was dimly aware that she would probably have a crashing headache the following morning. 'Sort of.'

'Sort of? Don't go coy on me, Aggie. How can people be *sort of* dead?'

Stripped bare of all the half-truths that had somehow been told to him over a period of time, Aggie resigned herself to telling him the unvarnished truth now about their background. He could do whatever he liked with the information, she thought recklessly. He could try to buy them off, could shake his head in disgust at being in the company of someone so far removed from himself. She should never have let her brother and Maria talk her into painting a picture that wasn't completely accurate.

A lot of that had stemmed from her instinctive need to protect Mark, to do what was best for him. She had let herself be swayed by her brother being in love for the first time, by Maria's tactful downplaying of just how protective her family was and why... And she also couldn't deny that Luiz had rubbed her up the wrong way from the very beginning. It hadn't been hard to swerve round the truth, pulling out pieces of it here and there, making sure to nimbly skip over the rest. He was so arrogant. He almost deserved it!

'We never knew our father,' she now admitted grudgingly. 'He disappeared after I was born, and continued showing up off and on, but he finally did a runner when Mum became pregnant with Mark.'

'He did a runner...'

'I'll bet you haven't got a clue what I'm talking about, Luiz.'

'It's hard for me to get my head around the concept of a father abandoning his family,' Luiz admitted.

'You're lucky,' Aggie told him bluntly and Luiz looked at her with dry amusement.

'My life was prescribed,' he found himself saying. 'Often it was not altogether ideal. Carry on.'

Aggie wanted to ask him to expand, to tell her what he meant by a 'prescribed life'. From the outside looking in, all she could see was perfection for him: a united, large family, exempt from all the usual financial headaches, with everyone able to do exactly what they wanted in the knowledge that if they failed there would always be a safety net to catch them.

'What else is there to say? I was nine when Mum died.' She looked away and stared off at the open fire. The past was not a place she revisited with people but she found that she was past resenting what he knew about her. He would never change his mind about the sort of person he imagined she was, but that didn't mean that she had to accept all his accusations without a fight.

'How did she die?'

'Do you care?' Aggie asked, although half-heartedly. 'She was killed in an accident returning from work. She had a job at the local supermarket and she was walking home when she was hit by a drunk-driver. There were no relatives, no one to take us in, and we were placed in a children's home. A wonderful place with a wonderful couple running it who saw us both through our bad times; we couldn't have hoped for a happier upbringing, given the circumstances. So please don't feel sorry for either of us.' The sandwiches were delicious but her appetite had nosedived.

'I'm sorry about your mother.'

'Are you?' But she was instantly ashamed of the

bitterness in her voice. 'Thank you. It was a long time ago.' She gave a dry, self-deprecating laugh. 'I expect all this information is academic because you've already made your mind up about us. But you can see why it wouldn't have made for a great opening conversation…especially when I knew from the start that the only reason you'd bothered to ask Maria out with us was so that you could check my brother out.'

Normally, Luiz cared very little about what other people thought of him. It was what made him so straightforward in his approach to tackling difficult situations. He never wasted time beating about the bush. Now, he felt an unaccustomed dart of shame when he thought back to how unapologetic he had been on every occasion he had met them, how direct his questions had been. He had made no attempt to conceal the reason for his sudden interest in his niece. He hadn't been overtly hostile but Aggie, certainly, was sharp enough to have known exactly what his motives were. So could he really blame her if she hadn't launched into a sob story about her deprived background?

Strangely, he felt a tug of admiration for the

way she had managed to forge a path for herself through difficult circumstances. It certainly demonstrated the sort of strength of personality he had rarely glimpsed in the opposite sex. He grimaced when he thought of the women he dated. Chloe might be beautiful but she was also colourless and unambitious…just another cover girl born with a silver spoon in her mouth, biding her time at a fairly pointless part-time job until a rich man rescued her from the need to pretend to work at all.

'So where was this home?'

'Lake District,' Aggie replied with a little shrug. She looked into those deep, deep, dark eyes and her mouth went dry.

'Hence you said that they went somewhere that had sentimental meaning for you.'

'Do you remember everything that people say to you?' Aggie asked irritably and he shot her one of those amazing, slow smiles that did strange things to her heart rate.

'It's a blessing and a curse. You blush easily. Do you know that?'

'That's probably because I feel awkward here

with you,' Aggie retorted, but on cue she could feel her face going red.

'No idea why.' Luiz pushed himself away from the table and stretched out his legs to one side. He noticed that they had managed to work their way through nearly two bottles of wine. 'We're having a perfectly civilised conversation. Tell me why you decided to move to London.'

'Tell me why *you* did.'

'I took over an empire. The London base needed expanding. I was the obvious choice. I went to school here. I understand the way the people think.'

'But did you *want* to settle here? I mean, it must be a far cry from Brazil.'

'It works for me.'

He continued looking at her as what was left of the sandwiches were cleared away and coffee offered to them. Considering the hour, their landlady was remarkably obliging, waving aside Aggie's apologies for arriving at such an inconvenient time, telling them that business was to be welcomed whatever time it happened to arrive. Beggars couldn't be choosers.

But neither of them wanted coffee. Aggie was

so tired that she could barely stand. She was also tipsy; too much wine on an empty stomach.

'I'm going to go outside for a bit,' she said. 'I think I need to get some fresh air.'

'You're going outside in *this* weather?'

'I'm used to it. I grew up with snow.' She stood up and had to steady herself and breathe in deeply.

'I don't care if you grew up running wild in the Himalayas, you're not going outside, and not because I don't think that you can handle the weather. You're not going outside because you've had too much to drink and you'll probably pass out.'

Aggie glared at him and gripped the table. God, her head was swimming, and she knew that she really ought to get to bed, do just as he said. But there was no way that she was going to allow him to dictate her movements on top of everything else.

'Don't tell me what I can and can't do, Luiz Montes!'

He looked at her in silence and then shrugged. 'And do you intend to go out without a coat, because you're used to the snow?'

'Of course not!'

'Well, that's a relief.' He stood up and shoved his hands in the pockets of his trousers. 'Make sure you have a key to get back in,' he told her. 'I think we've caused our obliging landlady enough inconvenience for one night without having to get her out of bed to let you in because you've decided to take a walk in driving snow.'

Out of the corner of his eye, he saw Mrs Bixby, the landlady, heading towards them like a ship in full sail. But when she began expressing concern about Aggie's decision to step outside for a few minutes, Luiz shook his head ever so slightly.

'I'm sure Agatha is more than capable of taking care of herself,' he told Mrs Bixby. 'But she will need a key to get back in.'

'I expect you want me to thank you,' Aggie hissed, once she was in possession of the front-door key and struggling to get her arms into her coat. Now that she was no longer supporting herself against the dining-room table, her light-headedness was accompanied by a feeling of nausea. She also suspected that her words were a little slurred even though she was taking care to enunciate each and every syllable very carefully.

'Thank me for what?' Luiz walked with her to the front door. 'Your coat's not done up properly.' He pointed to the buttons which she had failed to match up properly, and then he leaned against the wall and watched as she fumbled to try and remedy the oversight.

'Stop staring at me!'

'Just making sure that you're well wrapped up. Would you like to borrow my scarf? No bother for me to run upstairs and get it for you.'

'I'm absolutely fine.' A wave of sickness washed over her as she tilted her head to look him squarely in the face.

Very hurriedly, she let herself out of the house while Luiz turned to Mrs Bixby and grinned. 'I intend to take up residence in the dining room. I'll sit by the window and make sure I keep an eye on her. Don't worry; if she's not back inside in under five minutes, I'll forcibly bring her in myself.'

'Coffee while you wait?'

'Strong, black would be perfect.'

He was still grinning as he manoeuvred a chair so that he could relax back and see her as she stood still in the snow for a few seconds, breathing in deeply from the looks of it, before tramping in circles on the front lawn. He couldn't imagine her leaving the protective circle of light and striking out for an amble in the town. The plain truth was that she had had a little too much to drink. She had been distinctly green round the gills when she had stood up after eating a couple of sandwiches, although that was something she would never have admitted to.

Frankly, Luiz had no time for women who drank, but he could hardly blame her. Neither of them had been aware of how much wine had been consumed. She would probably wake up with a headache in the morning, which would be a nuisance, as he wanted to leave at the crack of dawn, weather permitting. But that was life.

He narrowed his eyes and sat forward as she became bored with her circular tramping and began heading towards the little gate that led out towards the street and the town.

Without waiting for the coffee, he headed for the front door, only pausing on the way to tell Mrs Bixby that he'd let himself back in.

She'd vanished from sight and Luiz cursed fluently under his breath. Without a coat it was freezing and he was half-running when he saw her staggering up the street with purpose before pausing to lean against a lamp post, head buried in the crook of her elbow.

'Bloody woman,' he muttered under his breath. He picked up speed as much as he could and reached her side just in time to scoop her up as she was about to slide to the ground.

Aggie shrieked.

'Do you intend to wake the entire town?' Luiz began walking as quickly as he could back to the bed and breakfast. Which, in snow that was fast settling, wasn't very quickly at all.

'Put me down!' She pummelled ineffectively at his chest but soon gave up because the activity made her feel even more queasy.

'Now, that has to be the most stupid thing ever to have left your lips.'

'I said put me *down*!'

'If I put you down, you wouldn't be able to get back up. You don't honestly think I missed the fact that you were hanging onto that lamp post for dear life, do you?'

'I don't need rescuing by you!'

'And I don't need to be out here in freezing

weather playing the knight in shining armour! Now shut up!'

Aggie was so shocked by that insufferably arrogant command that she shut up.

She wouldn't have admitted it in a million years but it felt good to be carried like this, because her legs had been feeling very wobbly. In fact, she really had been on the point of wanting to sink to the ground just to take the weight off them before he had swept her off her feet.

She felt him nudge the front door open with his foot, which meant that it had been left ajar. It was humiliating to think of Mrs Bixby seeing her like this and she buried herself against Luiz, willing herself to disappear.

'Don't worry,' Luiz murmured drily in her ear. 'Our friendly landlady is nowhere to be seen. I told her to go to bed, that I'd make sure I brought you in in one piece.'

Aggie risked a glance at the empty hall and instructed him to put her down.

'That dumb suggestion again. You're drunk and you need to get to bed, which is what I told you before you decided to prove how stubborn you could be by ignoring my very sound advice.'

'I am not *drunk*. I am *never* drunk.' She was alarmed by a sudden need to hiccup, which she thankfully stifled. 'Furthermore, I am *more than* capable of making my own way upstairs.'

'Okay.' He released her fast enough for her to feel the ground rushing up to meet her and she clutched his jumper with both hands and took a few deep breaths. 'Still want to convince me that you're *more than capable* of making your own way upstairs?'

'I hate you!' Aggie muttered as he swept her back up into his arms.

'You have a tendency to be repetitive,' Luiz murmured, and he didn't have to see her face to know that she was glaring at him. 'And I'm surprised and a little offended that you hate me for rescuing you from almost certainly falling flat on your face in the snow and probably going to sleep. As a teacher, you should know that that is the most dangerous thing that could happen, passing out in the snow. While under the influence of alcohol. Tut, tut, tut. You'd be struck off the responsible-teacher register if they ever found out about that. Definitely not a good example to set for impressionable little children, seeing their teacher the worse for wear...'

'Shut up,' Aggie muttered fiercely.

'Now, let's see. Forgotten which room is yours... Oh, it's coming back to me—the only one left with the *en suite*! Fortuitous, because you might be needing that...'

'Oh be quiet,' Aggie moaned. 'And hurry up! I think I'm going to be sick.'

CHAPTER FOUR

SHE made it to the bathroom in the nick of time and was horribly, shamefully, humiliatingly, wretchedly sick. She hadn't bothered to shut the door and she was too weak to protest when she heard Luiz enter the bathroom behind her.

'Sorry,' she whispered, hearing the flush of the toilet and finding a toothbrush pressed into her hand. While she was busy being sick, he had obviously rummaged through her case and located just the thing she needed.

She shakily cleaned her teeth but lacked the energy to tell him to leave.

Nor could she look at him. She flopped down onto the bed and closed her eyes as he drew the curtains shut, turned off the overhead light and began easing her boots off.

Luiz had never done anything like this before. In fact, he had never been in the presence of a woman quite so violently sick after a bout of excessive drinking and, if someone had told him that one day he would be taking care of such a woman, he would have laughed out loud. Women who were out of control disgusted him. An out-of-control Chloe, shouting hysterically down the phone, sobbing and shrieking and cursing him, had left him cold. He looked at Aggie, who now had her arm covering her face, and wondered why he wasn't disgusted.

He had wet a face cloth; he mopped her forehead and heard her sigh.

'So I guess I should be thanking you,' she said, without moving the hand that lay across her face.

'You could try that,' Luiz agreed.

'How did you know where to find me?'

'I watched you from the dining room. I wasn't going to let you stay out there for longer than five minutes.'

'Because, of course, you know best.'

'Staggering in the dark in driving snow when you've had too much to drink isn't a good idea in anyone's eyes,' Luiz said drily.

'And I don't suppose you'll believe me when I tell you that this is the first time I've ever... ever...done this?'

'I believe you.'

Aggie lowered her protective arm and looked at him. Her eyes felt sore, along with everything else, and she was relieved that the room was only lit by the small lamp on the bedside table.

'You do?'

'It's my fault. I should have said no to that second bottle of wine. In fact, I was barely aware of it being brought.' He shrugged. 'These things happen.'

'But I don't suppose they ever happen to you,' Aggie said with a weak smile. 'I bet you don't drink too much and stagger all over the place and then end up having to be helped up to bed like a baby.'

Luiz laughed. 'No, can't say I remember the last time that happened.'

'And I bet you've never been in the company of a woman who's done that.'

No one would dare behave like that in my presence, was what he could have said, except he was disturbed to find that that would have made him sound like a monster.

'No,' he said flatly. 'And now I'm going to go

and get you some painkillers. You're going to need them.'

Aggie yawned and looked at him drowsily. She had a sudden, sharp memory of how it had felt being carried by him. He had lifted her up as though she weighed nothing and his chest against her slight frame had been as hard as steel. He had smelled clean, masculine and woody.

'Yes. Thank you,' she said faintly. 'And once again, I'm so sorry.'

'Stop apologising.' Luiz's tone was abrupt. Was he really so controlling that women edited their personalities just to be with him; sipped their wine but left most of it and said no to dessert because they were afraid that he might pass judgement on them as being greedy or uncontrolled? He had broken off with Chloe and had offered her no explanation other than that she would be 'better off without him'. Strictly speaking, true. But he knew that, in the face of her hysterics, he had been impatient, short-tempered and dismissive. He had always taken it as a given that women would go out of their way to please them, just as he had always taken it as a given that he led a life of moving on; that, however hard they tried, one day it would just be time for him to end it.

Aggie bristled at his obvious displeasure at her repeated apology. God, what must he think of her? The starting point of his opinions had been low enough, but they would be a hundred times lower now—except when the starting point was gold-digger, then how much lower could they get?

She was suddenly too tired to give it any more thought. She half-sat up when he approached with a glass of water. She obediently swallowed two tablets and was reassured that she would be right as rain in the morning. More or less.

'Thanks,' Aggie said glumly. 'And please wake me up first thing.'

'Of course.' Luiz frowned, impatient at the sudden burst of unwelcome introspection which had left him questioning himself.

Aggie fell asleep with that frown imprinted on her brain. It was confusing that someone she didn't care about should have any effect on her whatsoever, but he did.

She vaguely thought that things would be back to normal in the morning. She would dislike him.

He would stop being three-dimensional and she would cease to be curious about him.

When she groggily came to, her head was thumping, her mouth tasted of cotton wool and Luiz was slumped in a chair he had pulled and positioned next to her bed. He was fully clothed.

For a few seconds, Aggie didn't take it in, then she struggled up and nudged him.

'What are *you* doing here?'

Belatedly she realised that, although the duvet was tucked around her, she was trouserless and jumperless; searing embarrassment flooded through her.

'I couldn't leave you in the state you were in.' Luiz pressed his eyes with his fingers and then raked both hands through his tousled hair before looking at her.

'I wasn't *in a state*. I...yes...I was...sick but then I fell asleep.'

'You were sick again,' Luiz informed her. 'And that's not taking into account raging thirst and demands for more tablets.'

'Oh God.'

'Sadly, God wasn't available, so it was up to me to find my way down to the kitchen for orange juice because you claimed that any more water would make you feel even more sick. I also had to deal with a half-asleep temper tantrum when I refused to double the dose of painkillers...'

Aggie looked at him in horror.

'Then you said that you were hot.'

'I didn't.'

'You threw off the quilt and started undressing.'

Aggie groaned and covered her face with her hands.

'But, gentleman that I am, I made sure you didn't completely strip naked. I undressed you down to the basics and you fell back asleep.'

Luiz watched her small fingers curl around the quilt cover. He imagined she would be going through mental hell but she was too proud to let it show. Had he ever met anyone like her in his life before? He'd almost forgotten the reason she was with him. She seemed to have a talent for running circles round his formidable single-mindedness and it wasn't just now that they had been thrown together. No, it had happened before. Some passing remark he might have made to which she had taken instant offence, dug her heels in and proceeded to argue with him until he'd forgotten the presence of other people.

'Well...thank you for that. I...I'd like to get changed now.' She addressed the wall and the dressing table in front of her, and heard him slap his thighs with his hands and stand up. 'Did you manage to get any sleep at all?'

'None to speak of,' Luiz admitted.

'You must be exhausted.'

'I don't need much sleep.'

'Well, perhaps you should go and grab a few hours before we start on the last leg of this journey.' It would be nice if the ground could do her a favour and open up and swallow her whole.

'No point.'

Aggie looked at him in consternation. 'What do you mean that there's no point? It would be downright foolhardy for you to drive without sleep, and I can't share any of the driving with you.'

'We've covered that. There's no point because it's gone two-thirty in the afternoon, it's already dark and the snow's heavier.' Luiz strode towards the window and pulled back the curtains to reveal never-ending skies the colour of lead, barely visible behind dense, relentlessly falling snow. 'It would be madness to try and get anywhere further in weather like this. I've already booked the rooms for at least another night. Might be more.'

'You can't!' Aggie sat up, dismayed. 'I thought I'd be back at work on Monday! I can't just *disappear*. This is the busiest time of the school year!'

'Too bad,' Luiz told her flatly. 'You're stuck. There's no way I intend to turn around and try and get back to London. And, while you're busy worrying about missing a few classes and the Nativity play, spare a thought for me. I didn't think that I'd be covering half the country in driving snow in an attempt to rescue my niece before she does something stupid.'

'Meaning that your job's more important than mine?' Aggie was more comfortable with this: an argument. Much more comfortable than she was with feverishly thinking about him undressing her, taking care of her, putting her to bed and playing the good guy. 'Typical! Why is it that rich people always think that what they do is more important than what everyone else does?' She glared at him as he stood by the door, impassively watching her.

For one blinding moment, it occurred to her that she was in danger of seeing beyond the obvious differences between them to the man underneath. If she could list all the things she disliked about him on paper, it would be easy to keep her distance and to fill the spaces between them with hostility and resentment. But to do that would be to fall into the trap of being as black-and-white in her opinions as she had accused him of being.

She paled and her heartbeat picked up in nervous confusion. Had he been working his charm on her from the very beginning? When he had drawn grudging laughs from her and held her reluctantly spellbound with stories of his experiences in foreign countries; when he had engaged her interest in politics and world affairs, while Maria and Mark had been loved up and whispering to each other, distracted by some shared joke they couldn't possibly resist. Had she already begun to see beyond the cardboard cut-out she wanted him to be?

And, stuck together in a car with him, here in this bed and breakfast. Would an arrogant, pompous, single-minded creep really have helped her the way he had the night before, not laughing once at her inappropriate behaviour? Keeping watch over her even though it meant that he hadn't got a wink of sleep? She had to drag out the recollection that he had offered her money in return for his niece; that he was going to offer her brother money to clear off; that liking or not liking someone was not something that mattered to him because he was like a juggernaut when it came to getting exactly what he wanted. He had loads of charm when it suited him, but underneath the charm he was ruthless, heartless and emotionless.

She felt a lot calmer once that message had got to her wayward, rebellious brain and imprinted itself there.

'Well?' she persisted scornfully, and Luiz raised his eyebrows wryly.

'I take it you're angling for a fight. Is this because you feel embarrassed about what happened last night? If it is, then there's really no need. Like I said…these things happen.'

'And, like you also said, you've never had this experience in your life before!' Aggie thought that it would help things considerably if he didn't look so damn gorgeous standing there, even though he hadn't slept and should look a wreck. 'You've never fallen down drunk, and I'll bet that none of your girlfriends have either.'

'You're right. I haven't and they haven't.'

'Is that because none of your girlfriends have ever had too much to drink?'

'Maybe they have.' Luiz shrugged. 'But never in my presence. And, by the way, I don't think that my job is any better or worse than yours. I have a very big deal on the cards which is due to close at the beginning of next week. A takeover. People's jobs are relying on the closure of this deal, hence the reason why it's as inconvenient for me to be delayed with this as it is for you.'

'Oh,' Aggie said, flustered.

'So, if you need to get in touch with your school and ask them for a day or so off, then I'm sure it won't be the end of the world. Now, I'm going to have a shower and head downstairs. Mrs Bixby might be able to rustle you up something to eat.'

He closed the door quietly behind him. At the mention of food, Aggie's stomach had started to rumble, but she made sure not to rush her bath, to take her time washing her hair and using the drier which she found in a drawer in the bedroom. She needed to get her thoughts together. There was no doubt that the fast-falling snow would keep them in this town for another night. It wasn't going to be a case of a few hours on the road and then, whatever the outcome, goodbye to Luiz Montes for ever.

She was going to have his company for longer than she had envisaged and she needed to take care not to fall into the trap of being seduced by his charm. It amazed her that common sense and logic didn't seem to be enough to keep her mind on the straight and narrow.

Rooting through her depleted collection of clothes, she pulled out yet more jeans and a jumper under which she stuck on various layers, a vest, a long-sleeved thermal top, another vest over that...

Looking at her reflection in the mirror, she wondered whether it was possible to look frumpier. Her newly washed hair was uncontrollable, curling in an unruly tumble over her shoulders and down her back. She was bare of make-up because there seemed no point in applying any, and anyway she had only brought her mascara and some lip gloss with her. Her clothes were a dowdy mixture of blues and greys. Her only shoes were the boots she had been wearing because she hadn't foreseen anything more extended than one night somewhere and a meal grabbed on the hop, but now she wished that she had packed a little bit more than a skeleton, functional wardrobe.

Luiz was on the phone when she joined him in the sitting room but he snapped shut the mobile and looked at her as she walked towards him.

With all those thick, drab clothes, anyone could be forgiven for thinking that she was shapeless. She wasn't. He had known that from the times he had seen her out, usually wearing dresses in which she looked ill at ease and uncomfortable. But even those dresses had been designed to cover up. Only last night had he realised just how shapely she was, despite the slightness of her frame.

Startled, he felt the stirrings of an arousal at the memory and he abruptly turned away to beckon Mrs Bixby across for a pot of tea.

'Not for me.' Aggie declined the cup put in front of her. 'I've decided that I'm going to go into town, get some fresh air.'

'Fresh air. You seem to be cursed with a desire for fresh air. Isn't that what got you outside last night?'

But she couldn't get annoyed with him because his voice was lazy and teasing. 'This time I'm not falling over myself. Like I told you, I enjoy snow. I wish it snowed more often in London.'

'The city would grind to a standstill. If you're heading out, then I think I'll accompany you.'

Aggie tried to stifle the flutter of panic his suggestion generated. She needed to clear her mind. However much she lectured herself on all the reasons she had for hating him, there was a pernicious thread of stubbornness that just wanted to go its own merry way, reminding her of his sexiness, his intelligence, that unexpected display of consideration the night before. How was she to deal with that stubbornness if he didn't give her a little bit of peace and privacy?

'I actually intended on going on my own,' she said in a polite let-down. 'For a start, it would give you time to work. You always work. I remember you saying that to us once when your mobile phone rang for the third time over dinner and you took the call. Besides, if you have an important deal to close, then maybe you could get a head start on it.'

'It's Saturday. Besides, it would do me good to stretch my legs. Believe it or not, chairs don't make the most comfortable places to sleep.'

'You're not going to let me forget that in a hurry, are you?'

'Would you if you were in my shoes?'

Aggie had the grace to blush.

'No,' Luiz murmured. 'Thought not. Well, at least you're honest enough not to deny it.' He stood up, towering over her while Aggie stuffed her hands in the pockets of her coat and frantically tried to think of ways of dodging him.

And yet, disturbingly, wasn't she just a little pleased that he would be with her? For good or bad, and she couldn't decide which, her senses were heightened whenever he was around. Her heart beat faster, her skin tingled more, her pulse raced faster and every nerve ending in her seemed to vibrate.

Was that nature's way of keeping her on her toes in the face of the enemy?

'You'll need to have something to eat,' was the first thing he said when they were outside, where the brutal cold was like a stinging slap on the face. The snow falling and collecting on the already thick banks on the pavements turned the winter-wonderland scene into a nightmare of having to walk at a snail's pace.

Her coat was not made for this depth of cold and she could feel herself shivering, while in his padded Barbour, fashioned for arctic conditions, he was doubtless as snug as a bug in a rug.

'Stop telling me what to do.'

'And stop being so damned mulish.' Luiz looked down at her. She had rammed her woolly hat low down over her ears and she was cold. He could tell from the way she had hunched up and the way her hands were balled into fists in the pockets of the coat. 'You're cold.'

'It's a cold day. I like it. It felt stuffy inside.'

'I mean, your coat is inadequate. You need something warmer.'

'You're doing it again.' Aggie looked up at him and her breath caught in her throat as their eyes tangled and he didn't look away. 'Behaving,' she said a little breathlessly, 'as though you have all the answers to everything.' She was dismayed to find that, although she was saying the right thing, it was as if she was simply going through the motions while her body was responding in a different manner. 'I've been meaning to buy another coat, but there's hardly ever any need for it in London.'

'You can buy one here.'

'It's a bad time of the year for me,' Aggie muttered. 'Christmas always is.' She eyed the small town approaching with some relief. 'We exchange presents at school...then there's the tree and the food...it all adds up. You wouldn't understand.'

'Try me.'

Aggie hesitated. She wasn't used to confiding. She just wasn't built that way and she especially couldn't see the point in confiding in someone like Luiz Montes, a man who had placed her in an impossible situation, who was merciless in pursuit, who probably didn't have a sympathetic bone in his body.

Except, a little voice said in her head, *he took care of you last night, didn't he? Without a hint of impatience or rancour.*

'When you grow up in a children's home,' she heard herself say, 'even in a great children's home like the one I grew up in, you don't really have any money. Ever. And you don't get brand-new things given to you. Well, not often. On birthdays and at Christmas, Betsy and Gordon did their best to make sure that we all had something new, but most of the time you just make do. Most of my clothes had been worn by someone else before. The toys were all shared. You get into the habit of being very careful with the small amounts of money you get given or earn by doing chores. I still have that habit. We both do. You'll think it silly, but I've had this coat since I was seventeen. It only occurs to me now and again that I should replace it.'

Luiz thought of the women he had wined and dined over the years. He had never hesitated in spending money on them. None of those relationships might have lasted, but all the women had certainly profited financially from them: jewellery, fur coats, in one instance a car. The memory of it repulsed him.

'That must have been very limiting, being a teenager and not being able to keep up with the latest fashion.'

'You get used to it.' Aggie shrugged. 'Life could have been a lot worse. Look, there's a café.

You're right. I should have something to eat. I'm ravenous.' It also felt a little weird to be having this conversation with him.

'You're changing the subject,' he drawled as they began mingling with the shoppers who were out in numbers, undeterred by the snow. 'Is that something else you picked up growing up in a children's home?'

'I don't want to be cross-examined by you.' They were inside the café which was small and warm and busy, but there were spare seats and they grabbed two towards the back. When Aggie removed her gloves, her fingers were pink with cold and she had to keep the coat on for a little longer, just until she warmed up, while two waitresses gravitated, goggle-eyed, to Luiz and towards their table to take their order.

'I could eat everything on the menu.' Aggie sighed, settling for a chicken baguette and a very large coffee. 'That's what having too much to drink does for a girl. I can't apologise enough.'

'And I can't tell you how tedious it is hearing you continually apologise,' Luiz replied irritably. He glanced around him and sprawled back in the chair. 'I thought women enjoyed nothing more than talking about themselves.'

Aggie shot him a jaundiced look and sat back while her baguette, stuffed to bursting, was placed in front of her. Luiz was having nothing; it should have been a little embarrassing, diving into a foot-long baguette while he watched her eat, but she didn't care. Her stomach was rumbling with hunger. And stranded in awful conditions away from her home turf was having a lowering effect on her defences.

'I'll bet that really gets on your nerves,' Aggie said between mouthfuls, and Luiz had the grace to flush.

'I tend to go out with women whose conversations fall a little short of riveting.'

'Then why do you go out with them? Oh yes, I forgot. Because of the way they look.' She licked some tarragon mayonnaise from her finger and dipped her eyes, missing the way he watched, with apparent fascination, that small, unconsciously sensual gesture. Also missing the way he sat forward and shifted awkwardly in the chair. 'Why do you bother to go out with women if they're boring? Don't you want to settle down and get married? Would you marry someone who bored you?'

Luiz frowned. 'I'm a busy man. I don't have the time to complicate my life with a relationship.'

'Relationships don't have to complicate lives. Actually, I thought they were supposed to make life easier and more enjoyable. This baguette is delicious; thank you for getting it for me. I suppose we should discuss my contribution to this... this...'

'Why? You wouldn't be here if it weren't for me.'

He drummed his fingers on the table and continued to look at her. Her hair kept falling across her face as she leant forward to eat the baguette and, as fast as it fell, she tucked it behind her ear. There were crumbs by her mouth and she licked them off as delicately as a cat.

'True.' Aggie sat back, pleasantly full having demolished the baguette, and she sipped some of her coffee, holding the mug between both her hands. 'So.' She tossed him a challenging look. 'I guess your parents must want you to get married. At least, that's...'

'At least that's what?'

'None of my business.'

'Just say what you were going to say, Aggie. I've seen you half-undressed and ordering me to fetch you orange juice. It's fair to say that we've gone past the usual pleasantries.'

'Maria may have mentioned that everyone's waiting for you to tie the knot.' Aggie stuck her chin up defiantly because if he could pry into her life, whatever his reasons, then why shouldn't she pry into his?

'That's absurd!'

'We don't have to talk about this.'

'There's nothing *to* talk about!' But wasn't that why he found living in London preferable to returning to Brazil—because his mother had a talent for cornering him and pestering him about his private life? He loved his mother very much, but after three futile attempts to match-make him with the daughters of family friends he had had to draw her to one side and tell her that she was wasting her time.

'My parents have their grandchildren, thanks to three of my sisters, and that's just as well, as I have no intention of tying any knots any time soon.' He waited for her response and frowned when none was forthcoming. 'In our family,' he said abruptly, 'the onus of running the business, expanding it, taking it out of Brazil and into the rest of the world, fell on my shoulders. That's just the way it is. It doesn't leave a lot of time for pandering to a woman's needs. Aside from the physical.' He elaborated with a sudden, wolfish smile.

Aggie didn't smile back. It didn't sound like that great a trade-off to her. Yes, lots of power, status, influence and money, but if you didn't have time to enjoy any of that with someone you cared about then what was the point?

She suddenly saw a man whose life had been prescribed from birth. He had inherited an empire and he had never had any choice but to submit to his responsibility. Which, she conceded, wasn't to say that he didn't enjoy what he did. But she imagined that being stuck up there at the very top, where everyone else's hopes and dreams rested on your shoulders, might become a lonely and isolated place.

'Spare me the look of sympathy.' Luiz scowled and looked around for a waitress to bring the bill.

'So what happens when you marry?' she asked in genuine bewilderment, even though she was sensing that the conversation was not one he had any particular desire to continue. In fact, judging from the dark expression on his face, she suspected that he might be annoyed with himself for having said more than he wanted to.

'I have no idea what you mean by that.'

'Will you give over the running of your…er… company to someone else?'

'Why would I do that? It's a family business. No one outside the family will ever have direct control.'

'You're not going to have much time to be a husband, in that case. I mean, if you carry on working all the hours God made.'

'You talk too much.' The bill had arrived. He paid it, leaving a massive tip, and didn't take his eyes from Aggie's face.

She, in turn, could feel her temples begin to throb and her head begin to swim. His eyes drifted down to her full mouth, taking in the perfect, delicate arrangement of her features. Yes, he had looked at her before, had sized her up the first time they had met. But had he looked at her in the past like *this*? There was a powerful, sexual element to his lazy perusal of her face.

Or was she imagining it? Was it just his way of avoiding the conversation?

Her breasts were tingling and her thoughts were in turmoil. Aside from the obvious reasons, this man was not her type at all. She might appreciate his spectacular good looks in a detached way but on every other level she had never had time for men who belonged to the striped-suit brigade, whose *raison d'être* was to live and die for the sake of work. She liked them carefree and unconventional and creative, so why had her body reacted like that just then—with the unwelcome frisson of a teenager getting randy on her first date with the guy of her dreams? God, even worse, was it the first time she had reacted like that? Or had she contrived to ignore all those tell-tale signs of a woman looking at a man and imagining?

'Yes. You're right. I do.' Her breathing was shallow, her pupils dilated.

On a subliminal level, Luiz registered these reactions. He was intensely physical, and if he didn't engage in soul searching relationships with women he made up for that in his capacity to read them and just know when they were affected by him.

Usually, it was a simple game with a foregone conclusion, and the women who ended up in his bed were women who understood the rules of the game. He played fair, as far as he was concerned. He never promised anything, but he was a lavish and generous lover.

So what, he wondered, was *this* all about? What the hell was going on?

She was standing up, brushing some crumbs off her jumper and slinging back on the worn, too-thin coat, pulling the woolly hat low down on her head, wriggling her fingers into her gloves. She wasn't looking at him. In fact, she was doing a good job of making sure that she didn't look at him.

Like a predator suddenly on the alert, Luiz could feel something inside him shift gear. He fell in beside her once they were outside and Aggie, nervous for no apparent reason, did what she always did when she was nervous. She began talking, barely pausing to draw breath. She admired the Christmas lights a little too enthusiastically and paused to stand in front of the first shop they came to, apparently lost in wonder at the splendid display of household items and hardware appliances. Her heart was thumping so hard that she was finding it difficult to hold on to her thoughts.

How had they ended up having such an intensely personal conversation? When had she stopped keeping him at a distance? Why had it become so easy to forget all the things she should be hating about him? Was that the power of lust? Did it turn your world on its head and make you lose track of everything that was sensible?

Just admitting to being attracted to him made her feel giddy, and when he told her that they should be getting back because she looked a little white she quickly agreed.

Suddenly this trip seemed a lot more dangerous than it had done before. It was no longer a case of trying to avoid constant sniping. It was a case of trying to maintain it.

CHAPTER FIVE

BY THE Monday morning—after two evenings spent by Aggie trying to avoid all personal conversation, frantically aware of the way her body was ambushing all her good intentions—the relentless snow was beginning to abate, although not sufficiently for them to begin the last leg of their journey.

The first thing Aggie did was to telephone the school. As luck would have it, it was shut, with just a recorded message informing her that, due to the weather, it would remain shut until further notice. She didn't know if it was still snowing in London, but the temperatures across the country were still sub-zero and she knew from experience that, even if the snow had stopped, sub-zero temperatures would result in frozen roads and pavements, as well as a dangerously frozen playground. This routinely happened once or twice a year, although usually only for a couple of days at most, and Health and Safety were always quick to step in and advise closures.

Then she looked at the pitiful supply of clothes remaining in her bag and said goodbye to all thoughts of saving any money at all for the New Year.

'I need to go back into town,' she told Luiz as soon as she had joined him in the dining room, where Mrs Bixby was busy chatting to the errant guest who had returned the evening before and was complaining bitterly about his chances of doing anything of any use. Salesmen rarely appreciated dire weather.

'More fresh air?'

'I need to buy some stuff.'

'Ah. New coat, by any chance?' Luiz sat back, tilting his chair away from the table so that he could cross his legs.

'I should get another jumper…some jeans, maybe. I didn't think that we would be snowed in when we're not even halfway through this trip.'

Luiz nodded thoughtfully. 'Nor had I. I expect I'll be forced to get some as well.'

'And you're missing your…meetings. You mentioned that deal you needed to get done.'

'I've telephoned my guys in London. They'll cover me in my absence. It's not perfect, but it'll have to do. This evening I'll have a conference call and give them my input. I take it you've called the school?'

'Closed anyway.' She sat back as coffee was brought for them, and chatted for a few minutes with their landlady, who was extremely cheerful at the prospect of having them there longer than anticipated.

'So your school's closed. How fortuitous,' Luiz murmured. 'I've tried calling the hotel where your brother is supposed to be holed up with Maria and the lines are down.'

'So is there any point in continuing?' Aggie looked at him and licked her lips. 'They were only going to be there for a few days. We could get up there and find they've already caught the train back to London.'

'It's a possibility.'

'Is that all you have to say?' Aggie cried in an urgent undertone. *'It's a possibility?* Neither of us can afford to spend time away from our jobs on a possibility!' The thought of her cold, uncomfortable, Luiz-free house beckoned like a port in a storm. She didn't understand why she was feeling what she was, and the sooner she was removed from the discomfort of her situation the better, as far as she was concerned. 'You have important meetings to go to. You told me so yourself. Just think of all those poor people whose livelihoods depend on you closing whatever deal it is you have to close!'

'Why, Aggie, I hadn't appreciated how concerned you were.'

'Don't be sarcastic, Luiz. You're a workaholic. It must be driving you crazy being caught out like this. It would take us the same length of time to return to London as it would to get to the Lake District.'

'Less.'

'Even better!'

'Furthermore, we would probably be driving away from the worst of the weather, rather than into it.'

'Exactly!'

'Which isn't to say that I have any intention of returning to London without having accomplished what I've set out to do. When I start something, I finish it.'

'Even if finishing it makes no sense?'

'This is a pointless conversation,' Luiz said coolly. 'And why the sudden desperation to jump ship?'

'Like I said, I thought I would be away for one night, two at most. I have things to do in London.'

'Tell me what. Your school's closed.'

'There's much more to teaching than standing in front of the children and teaching them. There are lessons to prepare, homework to mark.'

'And naturally you have no computer with you.'

'Of course I haven't.' He wasn't going to give way. She hadn't really expected that he would. She had known that he was the type of man who, once embarked on a certain course, saw it through to the finish. 'I have an old computer. There's no way I could lug that anywhere with me. Not that I thought I'd need it.'

'I'll buy you a laptop.' To Luiz's surprise, it was out before he had had time to think over the suggestion.

'I beg your pardon?'

'Everyone needs a laptop, something they can take with them on the move.' He flushed darkly and raked his fingers through his hair. 'I'm surprised you haven't got one. Surely the school would subsidise you?'

'I have a school computer but I don't take it out of the house. It's not my property.' Aggie was in a daze at his suggestion, but underneath, a slow anger was beginning to build. 'And would the money spent on this act of generosity be deducted from my full and final payment when you throw cash at me and my brother to get us out of the way? Are you keeping a mental tally?'

'Don't be absurd,' Luiz grated. He barely glanced at the food that had been placed in front of him by Mrs Bixby who, sensing an atmosphere, tactfully withdrew.

'Thanks, but I think I'll turn down your kind offer to buy me a computer.' This was how far apart their lives were, Aggie thought. Her body might play tricks on her, make her forget the reality of their situation, but this was the reality. They weren't on a romantic magical-mystery tour and he wasn't the man of her dreams. She was here because he had virtually blackmailed her into going with him and, far from being the man of her dreams, he was cold, single-minded and so warped by his privileged background that it was second nature to him to buy people. He could, so why not? His dealings with the human race were all based on financial transactions. He had girlfriends because they were beautiful and amused him for a while. But what else was there in his life? And did he imagine that there was nothing money couldn't buy?

'Too proud, Aggie?'

'I have no idea what you're talking about.'

'You think I've insulted you by offering to buy you something you need. You're here because of me. You'll probably end up missing work because of me. You'll need to buy clothes because of me.'

'So are you saying that you made a mistake in dragging me along with you?'

'I'm saying nothing of the sort.' Luiz looked at her, frowning with impatience. More and more he was finding it impossible to believe that she could be any kind of gold-digger. What sane opportunist would argue herself out of a free wardrobe? A top-of-the-range laptop computer? 'Of course you had to come with me.' But his voice lacked conviction. 'It's possible you weren't involved in trying to set your brother up with my niece,' he conceded.

'So you *did* make a mistake dragging me along with you.'

'I still intend to make sure that your brother stays away from Maria.'

'Even though you must know that he had no agenda when he got involved with her?'

Luiz didn't say anything and his silence spoke louder than words. Of course, he would never allow Mark to marry his niece. None of his family would. The wealthy remained wealthy because they protected their wealth. They married other wealthy people. That was his world and it was the only world he understood.

It was despicable, so why couldn't she look at him with indifference and contempt? Why did she feel this tremendous physical pull towards him however much her head argued that she shouldn't? It was bewildering and enraging at the same time and Aggie had never felt anything like it before. It was as if a whole set of brand-new emotions had been taken out of a box and now she had no idea how to deal with them.

'You really do come from a completely different world,' Aggie said. 'I think it's very sad that you can't trust anyone.'

'There's a little more to it than that,' Luiz told her, irritated. 'Maria's mother fell in love with an American twenty years ago. That American was Maria's father. There was a shotgun wedding. My sister went straight from her marriage vows to the hospital to deliver her baby. Of course, my parents were concerned, but they knew better than to say anything.'

'Why were they concerned? Because he was an American?'

'Because he was a drifter. Luisa met him when she was on holiday in Mexico. He was a lifeguard at one of the beaches. She was young and he swept her off her feet, or so the story goes. The minute they were married, the demands began. It turned out that Brad James had very expensive tastes. The rolling estate and the cars weren't enough; he wanted a private jet, and then he needed to be bankrolled for ventures that were destined for disaster. Maria knows nothing of this. She only knows that her father was killed in a light-aeroplane crash during one of his flying lessons. Luisa never forgot the mistakes she made.'

'Well, I'm sorry about that. It must have been hard growing up without a father.' She bit into a slice of toast that tasted like cardboard. 'But I don't want anything from you and neither does my brother.'

'You don't want anything from anyone. Am I right?'

Aggie flushed and looked away from those dark, piercing eyes. 'That's right.'

'But I'm afraid I insist on buying you some replacement clothes. Accept the offer in the spirit in which it was intended. If you dislike accepting them to such an extent, you can chuck them in a black bin-bag when you return to London and donate them all to charity.'

'Fine.' Her proud refusal now seemed hollow and churlish. He was being practical. She needed more clothes through no fault of her own. He could afford to buy them for her, so why shouldn't she accept the offer? It made sense. He wasn't to know that she wasn't given to accepting anything from anyone and certainly not charitable donations. Or maybe he had an idea.

At any rate, if he wanted to buy her stuff, then

not only would she accept but she would accept with alacrity. It was better, wasn't it, than picking away at generosity, finding fault with it, tearing it to shreds?

With Christmas not far away, the town was once again bustling with shoppers, even though the snow continued falling. There was no convenient department-store but a series of small boutiques.

'I don't usually shop in places like this.' Aggie dithered outside one of the boutiques as Luiz waited for her, his hand resting on the door, ready to push it open. 'It looks expensive. Surely there must be somewhere cheaper?' He dropped his hand and stood back to lean against the shop front.

They had walked into town in silence. It had irritated the hell out of Luiz. Women loved shopping. So what if she had accepted his offer to buy her clothes under duress? The fact was, she was going to be kitted out, and surely she must be just a little bit pleased? If she was, then she was doing a damned good job of hiding it.

'And I've never stayed in a bed and breakfast before the one we're in now,' Luiz said shortly.

'You're fond of reminding me of all the things I'm ignorant of because I've been insulated by my background. Well, I'm happy to try them out. Have you heard me complain once about where we're staying? Even though you've passed sufficient acid remarks about me being unable to deal with it because the only thing I can deal with are five-star hotels.'

'No,' Aggie admitted with painful honesty, while her face burned. She wanted to cover her ears with her hands because everything he was saying had a ring of truth about it.

'So I'm taking it that there are two sets of rules here. You're allowed to typecast me, whilst making damned sure that you don't get yourself typecast.'

'I can't help it,' Aggie muttered uncomfortably.

'Well, I suggest you try. So we're going to go into that shop and you're going to try on whatever clothes you want and you're going to let me buy whatever clothes you want. The whole damned shop if it takes your fancy!'

Aggie smiled and then giggled and slanted an upwards look at him. 'You're crazy.'

In return, Luiz smiled lazily back at her. She

didn't smile enough. At least, not with him. When she did, her face became radiantly appealing. 'Compliment or not?' he murmured softly, and Aggie felt the ground sway under her feet.

'I'm not prepared to commit on that,' she told him sternly, but the corners of her mouth were still twitching.

'Come on.'

It was just the sort of boutique where the assistants were trained to be scary. They catered for rich locals and passing tourists. Aggie was sure that, had she strolled in, clad in her worn clothes and tired boots, they would have followed her around the shop, rearranging anything she happened to take from the shelves and keeping a close eye just in case she was tempted to make off with something.

With Luiz, however, shopping in an over-priced boutique was something of a different experience. The young girl who had greeted them at the door, as bug-eyed in Luiz's presence as the waitress had been on Saturday in the café, was sidelined and they were personally taken care of by an older woman who confided that she was the owner of the shop. Aggie was made to sit on the *chaise longe*, with Luiz sprawled next to her, as relaxed as if he owned the place. Items of clothing were brought out and most were immediately dismissed by him with a casual wave of the hand.

'I thought *I* was supposed to be choosing my own outfits,' Aggie whispered at one point, guiltily thrilled to death by this take on the shopping experience.

'I know what would look good on you.'

'I should get some jeans…' She worried her lower lip and inwardly fretted at the price of the designer jeans which had been draped over a chair, awaiting inspection. Belatedly, she added, 'And you don't know what would look good on me.'

'I know there's room for improvement, judging from the dismal blacks and greys I've seen you wear in the past.'

Aggie turned to him, hot under the collar and ready to be self-righteous. And she just didn't know what happened. Rather, she knew *exactly* what happened. Their eyes clashed. His, dark and amused… Hers, blue and sparking. Sitting so close to each other on the sofa, she could breathe him in and she gave a little half-gasp.

She knew he was going to kiss her even before she felt his cool lips touch hers, and it was as if she had been waiting for this for much longer than a couple of days. It was as if she had been waiting ever since the very first time they had met.

It was brief, over before it had begun, although when he drew back she found that she was still leaning into him, her mouth parted and her eyes half-closed.

'Bad manners to launch into an argument in a shop,' he murmured, which snapped her out of her trance, though her heart was beating so hard that she could scarcely breathe.

'You kissed me to shut me up?'

'It's one way of stopping an argument in the making.'

Aggie tried and failed to be enraged. Her lips were still tingling and her whole body felt as though it was on fire. That five-second kiss had been as potent as a red-hot branding iron. While she tried hard to conceal how affected she had been by it, he now looked away, the moment already forgotten, his attention back to the shop owner who had emerged with more handfuls of clothing, special items from the stock room at the back.

'Jeans—those three pairs. Those jumpers and that dress...not that one, the one hanging at the back.' He turned to Aggie, whose lips were tightly compressed. 'You look as though you've swallowed a lemon whole.'

'I would appreciate it if you would keep your hands to yourself!' she muttered, flinty-eyed, and Luiz grinned, unperturbed by this show of anger.

'I hadn't realised that my hands had made contact with your body,' he said silkily. 'If they had, you would certainly know about it. Now, be a good girl and try on that lot. Oh, and I want to see how you look in them.'

Aggie, the very last person on earth anyone could label an exhibitionist, decided that she hated parading in front of Luiz. Nevertheless, she couldn't deny the low-level buzz of unsettling excitement threading through her as she walked out in the jeans, the jumpers and various T-shirts in bright colours. He told her to slow down and not run as though she was trying out for a marathon. When she finally arrived at the dress, she held it up and looked at him quizzically.

'A dress?'

'Humour me.'

'I don't wear bright blues.' Nor did she wear silky dresses with plunging necklines that clung to her body like a second skin, lovingly outlining every single curve.

'This is a crazy dress for me to try on in the middle of winter,' she complained, walking towards him in the high heels which the sales assistant had slipped under the door for her. 'When it's snowing outside...'

Luiz could count on the fingers of one hand the times when he had ever been lost for words. He was lost for words now. He had been slouching on the low sofa, his hands lightly clasped on his lap, his long legs stretched out in front of him. Now he sat up straight and ran his eyes slowly up and down the length of her small but incredibly sexy body.

The colour of the dress brought out the amazing aquamarine of her eyes, and the cut of the stretchy, silky fabric left very little to the imagination when it came to revealing the surprising fullness of her breasts, the slenderness of her legs and the flatness of her stomach. He wanted to tell her to go back inside the dressing room and re-move her bra so that he could see how the dress looked without two white bra-straps visible on her narrow shoulders.

'We'll have the lot.' His arousal was sudden, fierce and painful and he was damned thank-ful that he could reach for his coat which he had draped over the back of the chair and position it on his lap. He couldn't take his eyes off her but he knew that the longer he looked, the more un-comfortable he was going to get.

'And we'd better get a move on,' he continued roughly. 'I don't want to be stuck out here in town for much longer.' He watched, mesmerised, at the sway of her rounded bottom as she walked back towards the changing room. 'And we'll have those shoes as well,' he told the shop owner, who couldn't do enough for a customer who had prac-tically bought half the shop, including a summer dress which she had foreseen having to hold in the store room until better weather came along.

'Thank you,' Aggie said once they were outside and holding four bags each. A coat had been one of the purchases. She was wearing it now and, much as she hated to admit it, it felt absolutely great. She hadn't felt a twinge of conscience as she had bid farewell to her old threadbare one in the shop, where it had been left for the shop owner to dispose of.

'Was it as gruelling an experience as you had imagined?' He glanced down and immediately thought of those succulent, rounded breasts and the way the dress had clung to them.

'It was pretty amazing,' Aggie admitted. 'But we were in there way too long. You want to get back. I understand that. I just...have one or two small things I need to get. Maybe we could branch off now? You could go and buy yourself some stuff.'

'You mean you don't want me to parade in front of you?' Luiz murmured, and watched with satisfaction the hectic flush that coloured her cheeks.

He hadn't expected this powerful sexual attraction. He had no idea where it was coming from. He wasn't sure when, exactly, it had been born and it made no sense, because she was no more his type than he, apparently, was hers. She was too argumentative, too mouthy and, hell, hadn't he started this trip with her in the starring role of gold-digger? Yet there was something strangely erotic and forbidden about his attraction, something wildly exciting about the way he knew she looked at him from under her lashes. He got horny just thinking about it.

Problem was…what was he to do with this? Where was he going to go with it?

He surfaced from his uncustomary lapse in concentration to find her telling him something about a detour she wanted him to make.

'Seven…what? What are you talking about?'

'I said that I'd like to stop off at Sevenoaks. It'll be a minor detour and I haven't been back there in over eighteen months.'

'What's Sevenoaks?'

'Haven't you been listening to a word I've been saying?' She assumed that, after the little jaunt in the clothes shop, his mind had now switched back to its primary preoccupation, which was work, and in that mode she might just as well have been saying 'blah, blah, blah'.

'In one ear, out the other,' Luiz drawled, marvelling that he could become so lost in his imagination that he literally hadn't heard a word she had been saying to him.

'Sevenoaks is the home we grew up in,' Aggie

repeated. 'Perhaps we could stop off there? It's only a slight detour and it would mean a lot to me. I know you're in a rush to get to Mark's hotel, but a couple of hours wouldn't make a huge difference, would it?'

'We could do that.'

'Right...well...thanks.' Suddenly she felt as though she wouldn't have minded spending the rest of their time in the town with him. In response to that crazy thought, she took a couple of small steps back, just to get out of that spellbinding circle he seemed to project around him, the one which, once entered, wreaked havoc with her thought processes. 'And I'll head off now and see you back at the bed and breakfast.'

'What are you going to buy?' Luiz frowned as he continued to stare down at her. 'I thought we'd covered all essential purchases. Unless there are some slightly less essential ones outstanding? There must be a lingerie shop of sorts somewhere...'

Aggie reacted to that suggestion as though she had been stung. She imagined parading in front of him wearing nothing but a lacy bra and pants and she almost gasped aloud.

'I can get my own underwear—thank you.' She stumbled over the words in her rush to get them out. 'And, no, I wasn't talking about that!'

'What, then?'

'Luiz, it's getting colder out here and I'd really like to get back to the bed and breakfast so...' She took a few more steps back, although her eyes remained locked with his, like stupid, helpless prey mesmerised by an approaching predator.

Luiz nodded, breaking the spell. 'I'll see you back there in...' he glanced at his watch. '...a couple of hours. I have some work to do. Let's make it six-thirty in the dining room. If we're to have any kind of detour, then we're going to have to leave very early in the morning, barring any overnight fall of snow that makes it impossible. So we'll get an early night.'

'Of course,' Aggie returned politely. She was gauging from the tone of his voice that, whatever temporary truces came into effect, nothing would deflect him from his mission. It suddenly seemed wildly inappropriate that she had thrilled to his eyes on her only moments before as she had provided him with his very own fashion show, purchased at great expense. She might have made a great song and dance about her scorn for money, her lack of materialism but, thinking about how she had strutted her stuff to those lazy, watchful eyes, she suddenly felt as though without even realising it she had been bought somehow. And not only that, she had enjoyed the experience.

'And I just want you to know...' Her voice was cooler by several degrees. 'That once we're back in London, I shall make sure that all the stuff you bought for me is returned to you.'

'Not this rubbish again!' Luiz dismissed impatiently. 'I thought we'd gone over all that old ground and you'd finally accepted that it wasn't a mortal insult to allow me to buy you a few essential items of clothing, considering we've been delayed on this trip?'

'Since when is a summer dress *an essential item of clothing*?'

'Climb out of the box, Aggie. So the dress isn't essential. Big deal. Try a little frivolity now and again.' He couldn't help himself. His gaze drifted down to her full lips. It seemed that even when she was getting on his nerves she still contrived to turn him on.

'You think I'm dull!'

'I think this is a ridiculous place to have an on-going conversation about matters that have already been sorted. Standing in the snow. The last thing either of us need is to succumb to an attack of winter flu.'

With her concerns casually swatted away, and her pride not too gently and very firmly put in its place, Aggie spun round on her heels without a backward glance.

She could imagine his amusement at her contradictory behaviour. One minute she was gracefully accepting his largesse, the next minute she was ranting and railing against it. It made no sense. It was the very opposite of the determined, cool, always sensible person she considered herself to be.

But then, she was realising that in his presence that determined, cool and always sensible person went into hiding.

Annoyed with herself, she did what she had to do in town, including purchasing some very functional underwear, and once back at the bed and breakfast she retreated up to her bedroom with a pot of tea. The landline at the hotel to which they were heading was still down and neither could she make contact with her brother on his mobile.

At this juncture, she should have been wringing her hands in worry at the prospect of the scene that would imminently unfold. She should have been depressed at the thought of Luiz doing his worst and bracing herself for a showdown that might result in her having to pick up the pieces. Her fierce protectiveness of her brother should have kicked in.

Instead, as she settled in the chair by the window with her cup of tea, she found herself thinking of Luiz and remembering the brush of his lips on hers. One fleeting kiss that had galvanised all the nerve-endings in her body.

She found herself looking forward to seeing him downstairs, even though she knew that it was entirely wrong to do so. Fighting the urge to bathe and change as quickly as possible, she took her time instead and arrived in the dining room half an hour after their agreed time.

She paused by the door and gathered herself. Luiz was in the clothes he had presumably bought after they had parted company, a pair of black jeans and a black, round-necked jumper. He had pushed his chair back and in front of him was his laptop, at which he was staring with a slight frown.

He looked every inch the tycoon, controlling his empire from a distance. He was a man who could have any woman he wanted. To look at him was to know that beyond a shadow of a doubt. So why was she getting into such a tizzy at the sight of him? He had kissed her to shut her up, and here she was, reacting as though he had swept her off her feet and transported her to his bed.

Luiz looked up and caught her in the act of staring. He shut his computer and in the space of a few seconds had clocked the new jeans, tighter than her previous ones, and one of the new, more brightly coloured long-sleeved T-shirts that clung in a way she probably hadn't noticed. It was warm in the dining room. No need for a thick jumper.

'I hope I'm not interrupting your work,' Aggie said, settling in the chair opposite him. There was a bottle of wine chilling in a bucket next to the table and she eyed it suspiciously. Now was definitely not the time to over-indulge.

'All finished, and you'll be pleased to know that the deal is more or less done and dusted.

Jobs saved. Happy employees. A few lucky ones might even get pay rises. What did you buy in town after you left me?'

He poured her some wine and she fiddled with the stem of the glass.

'A few toys,' Aggie confessed. 'Things to take to the home. The children don't get a lot of treats. I thought it would be nice if I brought some with me. I shall wrap them; it'll be hugely exciting for them. 'Course, I couldn't really splash out, but I managed to find a shop with nothing in it over a fiver.'

Luiz watched the animation on her face. This was what the women he dated lacked. They had all been beautiful. In some cases, they had graced the covers of magazines. But, compared to Aggie's mobile, expressive face, theirs seemed in recollection lifeless and empty. Like mannequins. Was it any wonder that he had tired of them so quickly?

'Nothing over a fiver,' he murmured, transfixed by her absorption in what she was saying.

Having pondered the mystery of why he found her so compellingly attractive, Luiz now concluded that it was because she offered more than a pretty face and a sexy body. He had always tired easily of the women he had gone out with. No problem there; he didn't want any of them hanging around for ever. But the fact that Chloe, who had hardly been long-term, could be classified as one of his more enduring relationships was saying to him that his jaded palate needed a change of scene.

Aggie might not conform to what he usually looked for but she certainly represented a change of scene. In every possible way.

'Why are you looking at me like that?' Aggie asked suspiciously.

'I was just thinking about my own excessive Christmases.' He spread his hands in a self-deprecating gesture. 'I am beginning to see why you think I might live in an ivory tower.'

Aggie smiled. 'Coming from you, that's a big admission.'

'Perhaps it's one of the down sides of being born into money.' As admissions went, this was one of his biggest, and he meant it.

'Well, if I'm being perfectly honest...' Aggie leaned towards him, her face warm and appreciative, her defence system instantly defused by a glimpse of the man who could admit to short-comings. 'I've always thought that pursuing money was a waste of time. 'Course, it's not the be-all and end-all, but I really enjoyed myself in that boutique today.'

'Which bit of it did you enjoy the most?'

'I've never actually sat on a chair and had anyone bring clothes to me for my inspection. Is that how it works with you?'

'I don't have time to sit on chairs while people bring me clothes to inspect,' Luiz said wryly. 'I have a tailor. He has my measurements and will make suits whenever I want them. I also have accounts at the major high-end shops. If I need anything, I just have to ask. There are people there who know the kind of things I want. Did you enjoy modelling the clothes for me?'

'Well…um…' Aggie went bright red. 'That was a first for me as well. I mean, I guess you wanted to see what you were paying for. That sounds awful. It's not what I meant.'

'I know what you meant.' He sipped some of his wine and regarded her thoughtfully over the rim of his glass. 'I would gladly have paid for the privilege of seeing you model those clothes for me,' he murmured. 'Although my guess is that you would have been outraged at any such suggestion. Frankly, it was a bit of a shame that there was any audience at all. Aside from myself, naturally. If it had been just the two of us, I would have insisted you remove your bra when you tried that dress on, for starters.'

Aggie's mouth fell open and she stared at him in disbelieving shock.

'You don't mean that,' she said faintly.

'Of course I do.' He looked surprised that she should disbelieve him.

'Why are you saying these things?'

'I'm saying what I mean. I don't know how it's happened, but I find myself violently attracted to you, and the reason I feel I can tell you this is because I know you feel the same towards me.'

'I do not!'

'Allow me to put that to the test, Aggie.'

This time there was nothing fleeting or gentle about his kiss. It wasn't designed to distract her. It was designed to prove a point, and she was as defenceless against its urgent power as she would have been against a meteor hurtling towards her at full tilt.

There was no rhyme or reason behind her reaction, which was driven purely on blind craving.

With a soft moan of surrender, she reached further towards him and allowed herself to drown in sensations she had never felt before.

'Point proved.' Luiz finally drew back but his hand remained on the side of her face, caressing her hot cheek. 'So the only remaining question is what we intend to do about this...'

CHAPTER SIX

AGGIE couldn't get to sleep. Luiz's softly spoken words kept rolling around in her mind. He had completely dropped the subject over dinner but the electricity had crackled between them and the atmosphere had been thick with unspoken thoughts of them in bed together.

Had she been that transparent all along? When had he realised that she was attracted to him? She had been at pains to keep that shameful truth to herself and she cringed to think how casually he had dropped it into the conversation as a given.

He was a highly sexual man and he would have no trouble in seeing sex between them as just the natural outcome of mutual attraction. He wouldn't be riddled with anxiety and he wouldn't feel as though he was abandoning his self-respect. For him, whatever the reasons for their trip, a sexual relationship between them would always be a separate issue which he would be able to compartmentalise. He was accustomed to relationships that didn't overlap into other areas of his life.

At a little after one, she realised that it was pointless trying to force herself to go to sleep.

She pulled on the dressing gown that had been supplied and was hanging on a hook on the bathroom door, shoved her feet in her bedroom slippers and headed for the door. One big disadvantage of somewhere as small as this was that there was no room-service for those times when sleep was elusive and a glass of milk was urgently needed. Mrs Bixby had kindly pointed out where drinks could be made after hours and had told them both that they were free to use the kitchen as their own.

Aggie took her time pottering in the kitchen. A cup of hot chocolate seemed a better idea than a glass of milk and it was a diversion to turn her mind to something other than turbulent thoughts of Luiz.

She tried without success to stifle her flush of pleasure at his admission that he had been looking at her.

Caught up between the stern lectures she was

giving herself about the craziness of his proposal, like uninvited guests at a birthday party were all sorts of troublesome questions, such as when exactly had he been looking at her and how often...?

None of that mattered, she told herself as she headed back up the stairs with the cup of hot chocolate. What mattered, what was *really* important, was that they get this trip over with as soon as possible and, whatever the outcome, she would then be able to get back to her normal life with its safe, normal routine. One thing that had been gained in the process was that he no longer suspected her of profiteering and she thought that he had probably dropped his suspicions of her brother as well. He still saw it as his duty to intervene in a relationship he thought was unacceptable, but at least there would be no accusations of opportunism.

However, when Aggie tried to remember her safe, normal routine before all these complications had arisen, she found herself thinking about Luiz. His dark, sexy face superimposed itself and squashed her attempts to find comfort in thinking about the kids at the school and what they would be getting up to in the run up to Christmas.

She didn't expect to see the object of her fevered thoughts at the top of the stairs. She was staring down into the mug of hot chocolate, willing it not to spill, when she looked up and there he was. Not exactly at the top of the stairs, but in the shadowy half-light on the landing, just outside one of the bedrooms, with just a towel round his waist and another hand towel slung over his neck.

Aggie blinked furiously to clear her vision and when the vision remained intact she made a strangled, inarticulate noise and froze as he strolled towards her.

'What are you doing here?' she asked in an accusing gasp as he reached to relieve her of the mug, which threatened to fall because her hands were trembling so much.

'I could ask *you* the same question.'

'I…I was thirsty.'

Luiz didn't answer. There were only five rooms on the floor and, if he hadn't known already, it wouldn't have been hard to guess which was hers because it was the only one with a light on. It shone through the gap under the door like a beacon and he beelined towards it so that she found herself with no choice but to follow him on unsteady legs.

The sight of his broad, bronzed back, those wide, powerful shoulders, made her feel faint. Her breasts ached. Her whole body was in the process of reminding her of the futility of denying the sexual attraction he had coolly pointed out hours earlier, the one she had spent the last few restless hours shooting down in flames.

He was in no rush. While her nerves continued to shred and unravel, he seemed as cool as a cucumber, standing back with a little bow to allow her to brush past him into the bedroom, where she abruptly came to a halt and stopped before he could infiltrate himself any further.

'Good night.'

Her cheeks were burning and she couldn't look him in the eye but she could imagine the little mocking smile on his mouth at her hoarse dismissal.

'So you couldn't sleep. I'm not sure if a hot drink helps with that. I have a feeling that's an old wives' tale...' Luiz ignored her good-night, although he didn't proceed into the bedroom. It was sheer coincidence that he had bumped into her on the landing, *pure bloody coincidence,* but didn't fate work in mysterious ways? The laws of attraction…wasn't that what they called it? He remembered some girlfriend waffling on about that years ago while he had listened politely and wondered whether she had taken leave of her senses. Yet here it was at work, because he had been thinking about the woman standing wide-eyed in front of him and had decided to cool his thoughts down with a shower, only to find her practically outside his bedroom door. Never did he imagine that he would thank providence for the basic provisions of a bed and breakfast with only two *en suites.*

'I was thirsty, I told you.'

'I was having trouble sleeping too,' Luiz said frankly, his dark eyes roving over her slight frame. Even at this ungodly hour, she still managed to look good. No make-up, hair all over the place but still bloody good. Good enough to ravish. Good enough to lift and carry straight off to that king-sized bed behind her.

He felt his erection push up, hard as steel, and his breath quickened.

Aggie cleared her throat and said something polite along the lines of, 'oh dear, that's a shame,' at which Luiz grinned and held out the mug so that she could take it.

'Would you like to know why?'

'I'm not really interested.'

'Aren't you?' Whatever she might say, Luiz had his answer in that fractional pause before she predictably shook her head.

He hadn't been off the mark with her. She wanted him as much as he wanted her. He could always tell these things. His mouth curved in lazy satisfaction as he played with the idea of eliminating the talking and just…kissing her. Just plunging his hands into that tangled blonde hair, pulling her towards him so that she could have proof of just how much he was turned on, kissing her until she begged him not to stop. He could feel her alertness and it hit him that he hadn't been turned on by any woman to this extent before in his life.

He had spent the past couple of hours with his computer discarded next to him on the bed while he had stared up at the ceiling, hands folded behind his head, thinking of her. He had made his intentions clear and then dropped the matter in the expectation that, once the seed was planted, it would take root and grow.

'I want you,' he murmured huskily. 'I can't make myself any clearer, and if you want to touch you can feel the proof for yourself.'

Aggie's heart was thudding so hard that she could barely think straight.

'And I suppose you always get what you want?' She stuck her disobedient hands behind her back.

'You tell me. Will I?'

Aggie took a deep breath and risked looking at him even though those dark, fabulous eyes brought on a drowning sensation.

'No.'

For a few seconds, Luiz thought that he had heard incorrectly. Had she just turned him down? Women never said no to him. Why would they? Without a trace of vanity, he knew exactly what he brought to the table when it came to the opposite sex.

'No,' he tried out that monosyllable and watched as she glanced down with a little nod.

'What do you mean, *no*?' he asked in genuine bafflement.

Aggie's whole body strained to be touched by him and the power of that yearning shocked and frightened her.

'I mean you've got it wrong,' she mumbled.

'I can feel what you're feeling,' he said roughly. 'There's something between us. A chemistry. Neither of us was asking for this but it's there.'

'Yes, well, that doesn't matter.' Aggie looked at him with clear-eyed resolve.

'What do you mean, *that doesn't matter*?'

'We're on opposite sides of the fence, Luiz.'

'How many times do I have to reassure you that I have conceded that you were innocent of the accusations I originally made?'

'That's an important fence but there are others. You belong to a dynasty. You might think it's fun to step outside the line for a while, but I'm not a toy that you can pick up and then discard when you're through with it.'

'I never implied that you were.' Luiz thought that, as toys went, she was one he would dearly love to play with.

'I may not be rich and I may have come from

a foster home, but it doesn't mean that I don't have principles.'

'And if I implied that you didn't, then I apologise.'

'And it doesn't mean that I'm weak either!' Aggie barrelled through his apology because, now that she had gathered momentum, she knew that it was in her interests to capitalise on it.

'Where are you going with that?' Luiz had the strangest feeling of having lost control.

'I'm not going to just *give in* to the fact that, yes, you're an attractive enough man and we happen to be sharing the same space...'

'I honestly can't believe I'm hearing this.'

'Yes, well, it's not my fault that you've lived such a charmed life that you've always got everything you wanted at the snap of a finger.'

Luiz looked down into those aquamarine eyes that could make a grown man go weak at the knees and shook his head in genuine incomprehension. Yes, okay, so maybe he had had a charmed life and maybe he had always got what he wanted, but this was crazy! The atmosphere between them was tangible and electric... What was wrong with two consenting adults giving in to what they both clearly wanted, whether she was brave enough to admit that or not?

'So...' Aggie took a couple of steps towards the door and placed her hand firmly on the door knob. As a support, it was wonderful because her legs felt like jelly. 'If you don't mind, I'm very tired and I really would like to get to bed now.'

She didn't dare meet his eyes, not quite, but lowering them was equally hazardous because she was then forced to stare at his chest with its dark hair that looked so aggressively, danger-ously *un-English*; at his flat, brown nipples and at the clearly defined ripple of muscle and sinew.

Luiz realised that he was being dismissed and he straightened, all the time telling himself that the woman, as far as he was concerned, was now history. He had never been rejected before, at least not that he could remember, and he would naturally accept the reality that he was being re-jected now, very politely but very firmly rejected. He had never chased any woman and he should have stuck with that format.

'Of course,' he said coldly, reaching to hold both ends of the towel over his shoulders with either hand.

Immediately, Aggie felt his cool withdrawal and hated it.

'I'll...er...see you tomorrow morning. What time do you want to leave?' This time she did look him squarely in the face. 'And will you still be taking that detour to...you know? I'd understand if you just want to get to our destination as quickly as possible...' But she would miss seeing Gordon and Betsy and all the kids; would miss seeing how everything was. Opportunities to visit like this were so rare. Frankly non-existent.

'And you question *my* motives?'

'What are you talking about?' It was Aggie's turn to be puzzled and taken aback at the harsh, scathing contempt in his voice.

'You have just made me out to be a guy who can't control his baser instincts—yet I have to question your choice of men because you seem to lump me into the category as the sort of man who gives his word on something only to retract it if it's no longer convenient!'

Hot colour flared in her cheeks and her mouth fell open.

'I never said...'

'Of course you did! Well, I told you that I would

make that detour so that you could visit your friends at your foster home and I intend to keep my promise. I may be many things, but I am honourable.'

With that he left, and Aggie fell against the closed door, like a puppet whose strings had been suddenly severed. Every bone in her body was limp and she remained there for a few minutes, breathing heavily and trying not to think about what had just taken place. Which, of course, was impossible. She could still breathe in his scent and feel his disturbing presence around her.

So he had made a pass at her, she thought, trying desperately to reduce it to terms she could grasp. Men had made passes at her before. She was choosy, accustomed to brushing them aside without a second thought.

But this man...

He got to her. He roused her. He made her aware of her sexuality and made her curious to have it explored. Even with all those drawbacks, all those huge, gaping differences between them...

But it was good that she had turned him down, she told herself. He had been open and upfront with her, which naturally she appreciated. Fall into bed because they were attracted to one another? Lots of other women would have grabbed the opportunity; Aggie knew that. Not only was he drop-dead gorgeous, but there was something innately persuasive and unbearably sexy about him. His arrogance, on the one hand, left her cold but on the other it was mesmeric.

Fortunately, she reasoned as she slipped back between the sheets and closed her eyes, she was strong enough to maintain her wits! That strength was something of which she could justifiably be proud. Yes, she might very well be attracted to him, but she had resisted the temptation to just give in.

With the lights out, the cup of hot chocolate forgotten and sleep even more elusive than it had been before she had headed down to the kitchen, Aggie wondered about those other women who had given in. He always got what he wanted. What had he wanted? And why on earth would he be attracted to a woman like her? She was pretty enough, but he could certainly get far prettier without the hassle of having any of them question him or argue with him or stubbornly refuse to back down.

Aggie was forced to conclude that there might be truth in the saying that a change was as good as a rest.

She was different, and he had assumed that he could just reach out and pluck her like fruit from a tree, so that he could sample her before tossing her aside to return to the other varieties of fruit with which he was familiar.

It was more troubling to think of her own motivations, because she was far more serious when it came to relationships. So why was she attracted to him? Was there some part of her, hitherto undiscovered, that really was all about the physical? Some hidden part of her, free of restraint, principles and good judgement, that she had never known existed?

More to the point, how on earth were they going to get along now that this disturbing ingredient had been placed in the mix? Would he be cool and distant towards her because she had turned him down?

Aggie knew that she shouldn't really care but she found that she did. Having seen glimpses of his charm, his intelligence, his sense of humour, she couldn't bear the thought of having to deal with his coolness.

She found that she need not have worried. At least, not as much as she had. She arrived for breakfast the following morning to find him chatting to Mrs Bixby. Although his expression was unreadable when he looked across to where she was standing a little nervously by the door, he greeted her without any rancour or hostility, drawing her into the conversation he had been having with the older woman. Something about the sights they could take in *en route*, which also involved convoluted anecdotes about Mrs Bixby's various relatives who lived there. She seemed to have hordes of family members.

Luiz looked at her not looking at him, deliberately keeping her face turned away so that she could pour all her energy into focusing on Mrs Bixby.

He had managed to staunch his immediate reaction to her dismissal of him. He had left her room enraged and baffled at the unpleasant novelty of having been beaten back. The rage and bafflement had been contained, as he had known they would be, because however uncharacteristic his behaviour had been in that moment, he was still a man who was capable of extreme self-control. He would have to shrug her off with the philosophical approach of you win a few, you lose a few. And, if he had never lost any, then this was as good a time as any to discover what it felt like. With a woman who was, in the bigger picture, an insignificant and temporary visitor to his life.

Outside, the snow had abated. Aggie had called the school, vaguely explained and then apologised for her absence. She hadn't felt all that much better when she had been told that there was nothing to rush back for because the term was nearly over.

'You know what it's like here,' the principal had chuckled. 'All play and not much work with just a week to go before the holidays. If you have family problems, then don't feel guilty about taking some time off to sort them out.'

Aggie did feel guilty, though, because the 'family problems' were a sluggish mix of her own problems which she was trying to fight a way through and it felt deceitful to give the impression that they were any more widespread than that.

She looked surreptitiously at Luiz and wondered what was going through his head. His deep, sexy voice wafted around her and made her feel a little giddy, as though she was standing on a high wire, looking a long way down.

Eventually, Mrs Bixby left and Luiz asked politely in a friendly voice whether she was packed and ready to go.

'We might as well take advantage of the break in the weather,' he said, tossing his serviette onto his plate and pushing his chair back. 'It's not going to last. If you go and bring your bag down, I'll settle up and meet you by reception.'

So this was how it was going to be, Aggie thought. She knew that she should have been pleased. Pleased that he was being normal. Pleased that there would not be an atmosphere between them. Almost as though nothing had happened at all, as though in the early hours of the morning she hadn't bumped into him on the landing, he hadn't strolled into her room wearing nothing but a couple of towels and he certainly hadn't told her that he wanted her. It could all have been a dream because there was nothing in his expression or in the tone of his voice to suggest otherwise.

There was genuine warmth in Mrs Bixby's hugs as she waved them off, and finally Aggie twisted back around in her seat and waited for something. Something to be said. Some indication that they had crossed a line. But nothing.

He asked for the address to the foster home and allowed her to programme the satnav, although her fingers fumbled and it took ages before the address was keyed in and their course plotted.

It would take roughly a few hours. Conditions were going to worsen slightly the further north they went. They had been lucky to have found such a pleasant place to stay a couple of nights but they couldn't risk having to stop again and make do.

Luiz chatted amiably and Aggie was horrified to find that she hated it. Only now was she aware of that spark of electricity that had sizzled between them because it was gone.

When the conversation faltered, he eventually tuned in to the local radio station and they drove without speaking, which gave her plenty of time alone with her thoughts.

In fact, she was barely aware of the motorway giving way to roads, then to streets, and she was shocked when he switched off the radio, stopped the car and said,

'We seem to be here.'

For the first time since they had started on this uncomfortable trip, Luiz was treated to a smile of such spontaneous delight and pleasure that it took his breath away. He grimly wondered whether there was relief in that smile, relief that she was to be spared more of his company. Whether she was attracted to him or not, she had made it perfectly clear that her fundamental antipathy towards him rendered any physical attraction null and void.

'It's been *such* a long time since I was here,' she breathed fervently, hands clasped on her lap. 'I just want to sit here for a little while and breathe it in.'

Luiz thought that anyone would be forgiven for thinking that she was a prodigal daughter, returned to her rightful palatial home. Instead, what he saw was an averagely spacious pebbledashed house with neat gardens on either side of a gravel drive. There was an assortment of outside toys on the grass and the windows of one of the rooms downstairs appeared to have drawings tacked to them. There were trees at the back but the foliage was sparse and unexciting.

'Same bus,' she said fondly, drawing his attention to a battered vehicle parked at the side. 'Betsy's always complained about it but I think she likes its unpredictability.'

'It's not what I imagined.'

'What did you imagine?'

'It seems small to house a tribe of children and teenagers.'

'There are only ever ten children at any one time and it's bigger at the back. You'll see. There's a conservatory—a double conservatory, where Betsy and Gordon can relax in the evenings while the older ones do their homework. They were always very hot on us doing our homework.' She turned to him and rested her hand on his forearm. 'You don't have to come in if you don't want to. I mean, the village is only a short drive away, and you can always go there for a coffee

or something. You have my mobile number. You
can call me when you get fed up and I'll come.'

'Not ashamed of me, by any chance, are you?'
His voice was mild but there was an edge to it
that took her aback.

'Of course I'm not! I was…just thinking of you.
I know you're not used to this…er…sort of thing.'

'Stop stereotyping me!' Luiz gritted his teeth
and she recoiled as though she had been slapped.

He hadn't complained once when they had been
at the bed and breakfast. In fact, he had seemed
sincerely impressed with everything about it, and
had been the soul of charm to Mrs Bixby. Aggie
was suddenly ashamed at the label she had casually dropped on his shoulders and she knew that,
whatever his circumstances of birth, and however little he was accustomed to roughing it, he
didn't deserve to be shoved in a box. If she did
that, then it was about *her* hang-ups and not his.

'I'm sorry,' she said quickly, and he acknowledged the apology with a curt nod.

'Take your time,' he told her. 'I'll bring that bag
in and don't rush. I'll watch from the sidelines.
I've just spent the last few hours driving. I can

do without another bout of it so that I can while away some time in a café.'

But he allowed her half an hour to relax in familiar surroundings without him around. He turned his mind to work, although it was difficult to concentrate when he was half-thinking of the drive ahead, half-thinking of her, wondering what it must feel like to be reunited with her pseudo-family. He had thought that she had stopped seeing him as a one-dimensional cardboard cut-out, but she hadn't, and could he blame her? He had stormed into her life like a bull in a china shop, had made his agenda clear from the beginning, had pronounced upon the problem and produced his financial solution for sorting it out. In short, he had lived down to all her expectations of someone with money and privilege.

He had never given a passing thought in the past as to how he dealt with other people. He had always been supremely confident of his abilities, his power and the reach of his influence. As the only son from a family whose wealth was bottomless, he had accepted the weight of responsibility for taking over his family's vast business concerns, adding to them with his own. Alongside that, however, were all the advantages that came with money—including, he reluctantly conceded, an attitude that might or might not be interpreted as arrogant and overbearing.

It was something that had never been brought to his notice, but then again he was surrounded by people who feared and respected him. Would they ever point out anything that might be seen as criticism?

Agatha Collins had no such qualms. She was in a league of her own. She didn't hold back when it came to pointing out the things she disliked about him although, he mused, she was as quick to apologise if she thought she had been unfair as she was to heap criticism when she thought she had a point. He had found himself in the company of someone who spoke her mind and damned the consequences.

On that thought, he slung his long body out of the car, collected the bag of presents which she had bought the day before and which he could see, as he idly peered into the bag, she had wrapped in very bright, jolly Christmas paper.

The door was pulled open before he had time to

hit the buzzer and he experienced a few seconds of complete disorientation. Sensory overload.

Noise; chaos; children; lots of laughter; the smell of food; colour everywhere in the form of paintings on the walls; coats hanging along the wall; shoes and wellies stacked by the side of the door. Somewhere roundabout mid-thigh area, a small dark-haired boy with enormous brown eyes, an earnest face and chocolate smeared round his mouth stared up at him, announced his name—and also announced that he knew who *he* was, because Aggie had said it would be him, which was why Betsy had allowed him to open the door, because they were *never* allowed to open the door. All of this was said without pause while the noise died down and various other children of varying sizes approached and stared at him.

Luiz had never felt so scrutinised in his life before, nor so lost for something to say. Being the focus of attention of a dozen, unblinking children's eyes induced immediate seizure of his vocal chords. Always ready with words, he cleared his throat and was immensely relieved when Aggie emerged from a room at the back, accompanied by a woman in her early seventies, tall, stern-looking with grey hair pulled back in a bun. When she smiled, though, her face radiated warmth and he could see from the reaction of the kids that they adored her.

'You look hassled,' Aggie whispered when introductions had been made. He was assured by Betsy that pandemonium was not usual in the house but she was being lenient, as it was Christmas, and that he must come and have something to eat, and he needn't fear that there would be any food throwing at the table.

'Hassled? I'm never hassled.' He slid his eyes across to her and raised his eyebrows. 'Overwhelmed might be a better word.'

Aggie laughed, relaxed and happy. 'It's healthy to be overwhelmed every so often.'

'Thanks. I'll bear that in mind.' He was finding it difficult to drag his eyes away from her laughing face. 'Busy place.'

'Always. And Betsy is going to insist on showing you around, I'm afraid. She's very proud of what she's done with the house.'

They had passed several rooms and were heading towards the back of the house where he could see a huge conservatory that opened out onto masses of land with a small copse at the back, which he imagined would be heaven for the kids here when it was summer and they could go outside.

'We won't be here long,' she promised. 'There's a little present-giving Christmas party. It's been brought forward as I'm here. I hope you don't mind.'

'Why should I?' Luiz asked shortly. It irked him immensely that, even though he had mentally decided to write her off, he still couldn't manage to kill off what she did to his libido. It was also intensely frustrating that he was engaging in an unhealthy tussle with feelings of jealousy. Everyone and everything in this place had the power to put a smile on her face. The kind of smile which she had shown him on rare occasions only.

He didn't understand this confused flux of emotion and he didn't like it. He enjoyed being in control of his life and of everything that happened around him. Agatha Collins was very firmly out of his control. If she were any other woman, she would have been flattered at his interest in her, and she wouldn't have hesitated to come to bed with him. It had been a simple, and in his eyes foolproof, proposition.

To have been knocked back was galling enough, but to have been knocked back only to find himself getting back to his feet and bracing himself for another onslaught on her defences bordered on unacceptable.

'I thought you might be bored,' Aggie admitted, flushing guiltily as his face darkened. 'Also...'

'Also what?'

'I know you're angry with me.'

'Why would I be angry with you?' Luiz asked coldly.

'Because I turned you down and I know I must have... You must have found that... Well, I guess I dented your ego.'

'You want me. I want you. I proposed we do something about that and you decided that you didn't want to. There's no question of my pride being dented.'

'I just can't approach sex in such a cold-blooded way.' Aggie was ashamed that after her show of will power she was now backtracking to a place from which she could offer up an explanation. 'You move in and out of women and...'

'And you're not a toy to be picked up and discarded when the novelty's worn off. I think you already made that clear.'

'So that's the only reason why I feel a little uncomfortable about asking you to put yourself out now.'

'Well, don't. Enjoy yourself. The end of the journey is just round the corner.'

CHAPTER SEVEN

'WE'RE never going to make it to Sharrow Bay tonight.'

They had been driving for a little under an hour and Luiz looked across to Aggie with a frown.

'Depends on how much more the weather deteriorates.'

'Yes, well, I don't see the point of taking risks on the roads. I mean, it's not as though Mark and Maria are going anywhere. Not in these conditions. We spent a lot longer than I anticipated at Sevenoaks and I apologise about that.'

Aggie didn't know how to get through the impenetrable barrier that Luiz had erected around himself. He had smiled, charmed and chatted with everyone at the home and had done so without a flicker of tension, but underneath she could feel his coolness towards her. It was like an invisible force field keeping her out and she hated it.

'I hope you didn't find it too much of a chore.'

She tried again to revive a conversation that threatened to go in the same direction as the last few she had initiated—slap, bang into a brick wall of Luiz's disinterest.

Her pride, her dignity and her sense of moral self-righteousness at having rightly turned down a proposal for no-strings sex for a day or two had disintegrated, leaving in its wake the disturbing realisation that she had made a terrible mistake. Why hadn't she taken what was on offer? Since when did sex have to lead to a serious commitment? There was no tenderness, and he would never whisper sweet nothings in her ear, but the power of the sexual pull he had over her cut right through all of those shortcomings.

Why shouldn't she be greedy for once in her life and just take without bothering about consequences and without asking herself whether she was doing the wrong thing or the right thing?

She had had three relationships in her life and on paper they had all looked as though they would go somewhere. They had been free-spirited, fun-loving, creative guys, nothing at all like Luiz. They had enjoyed going to clubs, attending protest marches and doing things on impulse.

And what had come of them? She had grown bored with behaviour that had ended up seeming juvenile and irresponsible. She had become fed up with the fact that plans were never made, with Saturdays spent lying in bed because none of them had ever shown any restraint when it came to drinking—and if she had tried to intervene she had been shouted down as a bore. With all of them, she had come to dread the aimlessness that she had initially found appealing. There had always come a point when hopping on the back of a motorbike and just riding where the wind took them had felt like a waste of time.

Luiz was so much the opposite. His self-control was formidable. She wondered whether he had ever done anything spontaneous in his life. Probably not. But despite that, or maybe because of it, her desire for him was liberated from the usual considerations. Why hadn't she seen that at the time? She had shot him down as the sort of person who could have relationships with women purely for sex, as if the only relationships worth considering were ones where you spent your time plumbing each other's depths. Except she had tried those and none of them had worked out.

'The kids loved you,' she persevered. 'And so did Betsy and Gordon. I guess it must have been quite an eye-opener, visiting a place like that. I'm thinking that your background couldn't have been more different.'

Like a jigsaw puzzle where the pieces slowly began to fit together, Luiz was seeing the background picture that had made Aggie the woman she had become. It was frustrating and novel to find himself in a position of wanting to chip away at the surface of a woman and dig deeper. She was suspicious, proud, defensive and fiercely independent. She had had to be.

'There's a hotel up ahead, by the way, just in case you agree with me that we need to stop. Next town along...' With every passing minute of silence from him, Aggie could feel her chances of breaking through that barrier slipping further and further out of reach.

'Is there? How do you know?' With her childhood home behind them, she was no longer the laughing, carefree person she had been there. Luiz could feel the tension radiating out of her, and if it were up to him he would risk the snow and plough on. The mission he had undertaken obviously had to reach a conclusion, but the cold-blooded determination that had initially fuelled him had gone. In its place was weary resignation for an unpleasant task ahead.

Aggie's heart picked up speed. How did she know about the hotel? Because she had checked it on the computer Betsy kept in the office. Because she had looked at Luiz as he had stood with his arms folded at the back of the room, watching Christmas presents being given out, and she had known that, however arrogant and ruthless he could be, he was also capable of generosity and understanding. He could easily have turned down her request for that detour. He was missing work, and the faster he could wrap up the business with Mark and his niece, the better for him. Yet not only had he put himself out but he had taken the experience in his stride. He had shown interest in everything Betsy and Gordon had had to say and had interacted with the kids who had been fascinated by the handsome, sophisticated stranger in their midst.

She had been proud of him and had wanted him so intensely that it physically hurt.

'I saw a sign for it a little way back.' She

crossed her fingers behind her back at that excusable white lie. 'And I vaguely remember Betsy mentioning ages ago that there was a new fancy hotel being built near here, to capture the tourist trade. It's booming in this part of the world, you know.'

'I didn't see any sign.'

'It was small. You probably missed it. You're concentrating on driving.'

'Wouldn't you rather just plough on? Get where we're heading? If we stick it out for another hour, we should be there, more or less.'

'I'd rather not, if you don't mind.' It suddenly occurred to her that the offer he had extended had now been withdrawn. He wasn't the sort of man who chased women. Having done so with her, he wasn't the sort of man who would carry on in the face of rejection. Did she want to risk her pride by throwing herself at him, when he now just wanted to get this whole trip over and done with so that he could return to his life?

'I have a bit of a headache coming on, actually. I think it must be all the excitement of today— seeing Gordon and Betsy, the children. Gordon isn't well. She only told me when we were about to leave. He's had some heart problems. I worry about what Betsy will do if something happens to him.'

'Okay. Where's the turning?'

'Are you sure? You've already put yourself out enough as it is.' Aggie held her breath. If he showed even a second's reluctance, then she would abandon her stupid plan; she would just accept that she had missed her chance; she would tell herself that it was for the best and squash any inclination to wonder...

'The turning?'

'I'll direct you.'

He didn't ask how she just happened to know the full address of the hotel, including the post code, in case they got lost and needed to use his satnav. After fifteen minutes of slow driving, they finally saw a sign—a real sign this time—and Aggie breathed a sigh of relief when they swung into the courtyard of a small but very elegant country house. Under the falling snow, it was a picture-postcard scene.

A few cars were in the courtyard, but it was obvious that business was as quiet here as it had been at Mrs Bixby's bed and breakfast. How many other people were slowly wending their way north by car in disastrous driving conditions? Only a few lunatics.

Her nerves gathered pace as they were checked in.

'Since this was my suggestion...' She turned to him as they walked towards the winding staircase that led to the first floor and up to their bedrooms. 'I insist on picking up the tab.'

'Have you got the money to pick up the tab?' Luiz asked. 'There's no point suggesting something if you can't carry it out.'

'I might not be rich but I'm not completely broke!' Nerves made her lash out at him. It wasn't the best strategy for enticing him into her bed. 'I'm doing this all wrong,' she muttered, half to herself.

'Doing what all wrong?' Luiz stopped and looked down at her.

'You're nothing like the guys I've been out with.'

'I don't think that standing halfway up the stairs in a hotel is the place for a soul-searching conversation about the men you've slept with.' He turned on his heels and began heading upstairs.

'I don't like you being like this with me!' Aggie caught up with him and tugged the sleeve of his jumper until he turned around and looked at her with impatience.

'Aggie, why don't we just go to our rooms, take some time out and meet in an hour for dinner? This has already turned into a never-ending journey. I've been away from work for too long. I have things on my mind. I don't feel inclined to get wrapped up in a hysterical, emotional conversation with you now.'

Luiz was finding it impossible to deal with his crazy obsession with her. He wondered if he was going stir crazy. Was being cooped up with her doing something to his self-control? It had not even crossed his mind, when he had made a pass at her, that she would turn him down. Was that why he had watched her with Betsy and Gordon and all those kids and the only thing he could think was how much he wanted to get her into his bed? Was he so arrogant, in the end, that he couldn't accept that any woman should say no to him?

The uneasy swirl of unfamiliar emotions had left him edgy and short-tempered. He would have liked to dismiss her from his mind the way he had always been able to dismiss all the inconveniences that life had occasionally thrown at him. He had always been good at that. Ruthlessness had always served him well. That and the knowledge that it was pointless getting sidetracked by things that were out of your control. Aggie sidetracked him and the last thing he needed was an involved conversation that would get neither of them anywhere. Womanly chats were things he avoided like the plague.

'I'm not being hysterical.' Aggie took a deep breath. If she backed away now, she would never do what she felt she had to do. Falling into bed with Luiz might be something she would never have contemplated in a month of Sundays, but then again she had never had to cope with a sexual attraction that was ripping her principles to shreds.

She had come to the conclusion that, whilst she knew it was crazy to sleep with a guy whose attitude towards women she found unnerving and amoral, not to sleep with him would leave her with regrets she would never be able to put behind her. And, if she was going to sleep with him, then she intended to have some control over the whole messy situation.

A lifetime of independence would not be washed away in a five-minute decision.

'I just want to talk to you. I want to clear the air.'

'There's nothing to clear, Aggie. I've done what you asked me to do, and I'm pleased you seemed to have had a good time seeing all your old friends, but now it's time to move on.'

'I may have made a mistake.'

'What are you talking about?'

'Can we discuss this upstairs? In your room? Or we could always go back downstairs to the sitting room. It's quiet there.'

'If you don't mind me changing while you speak, then follow me to my room, by all means.' He turned his back on her and headed up.

'So...' Once inside the bedroom, Luiz began pulling off his sweater which he flung on a chair by the window. Their bags had been brought up and deposited in their separate rooms and he began rummaging through his for some clothes.

'I never wanted to make this trip with you,'

Aggie began falteringly, and Luiz stilled and turned to look at her.

'If this is going to be another twenty minutes of recriminations, then let me tell you straight away that I'm not in the mood.' But, even as he spoke, he was seeing her tumble of fair hair and the slender contours of her body encased in a pair of the new jeans and deep burgundy jumper that was close-fitted and a lot sexier than the baggy jumpers she seemed to have stockpiled. Once again, his unruly lack of physical control made him grit his teeth in frustration. 'I'm also not in the mood to hear you make a song and dance about paying your own way.'

'I wasn't going to.' She pressed her back against the closed door.

'Then what was it you wanted to tell me?'

'I've never met anyone like you before.'

'I think,' Luiz said drily, 'you may have mentioned that to me in the past—and not in a good way—so unless you have something else to add to the mix then I suggest you go and freshen up.'

'What I mean is, I never thought I could be attracted to someone like you.'

'I don't do these kinds of conversations, Aggie.

Post mortems on a relationship are bad enough; post mortems on a non-relationship are a complete non-starter. Now, I'm going to have a shower.' He began unbuttoning his shirt.

Aggie felt the thrill of sudden, reckless excitement and a desperate urgency to get through to him. Despite or maybe because of her background she had never been a risk taker. From a young age, she had felt responsible for Mark and she had also gathered, very early on, that the road to success wasn't about taking risks. It was about putting in the hard work; risk taking was for people who had safety nets to fall into. She had never had one.

Even in her relationships, she had never strayed from what her head told her she should be drawn to. So they hadn't worked out. At no point, she now realised, had she ever concluded that maybe she should have sat back and taken stock of what her head had been telling her.

Luiz, so different from anyone she had ever known, who had entered her life in the most dubious of circumstances, had sent her into a crazy tailspin. She had found herself in terrifying new territory where nothing made sense and she had reacted by lashing out.

Before he could become completely bored with her circuitous conversation, Aggie drew in a deep breath. 'You made a pass at me and I'm sorry I turned you down.'

Luiz, about to pull off his shirt, allowed his arms to drop to his sides and looked at her through narrowed eyes. 'I'm not with you,' he said slowly.

Aggie propelled herself away from the safety of the door and walked towards him. Every step closer set up a tempo in her body that made her perspire with nervous tension.

'I always thought,' she told him huskily, 'that I could never make love to a guy unless I really liked him.'

'And the boyfriends you've had?'

'I really liked them. To start with. And please don't make it sound as though I've slept around; I haven't. I've just always placed a lot of importance on compatibility.'

'We all make mistakes.' At no point did it occur to Luiz that he would turn her away. The strength of his attraction was too overwhelming. He didn't get it, but he knew himself well enough to realise that it was something that needed sating. 'But the compatibility angle obviously didn't play out with you,' he couldn't help adding with some satisfaction.

'No, it didn't,' Aggie admitted ruefully. She sneaked a glance at him and shivered. He was just so gorgeous. Was it any wonder her will power was sapped? She would never have made a play for him. She would never have considered herself to be in the category of women he might be attracted to. It occurred to her that he only wanted her because she was different from the women he dated, but none of that seemed to matter, and she wasn't going to try and fight it.

'What happened?' Luiz strolled towards the king-sized four-poster bed and flopped down on it, his hands linked behind his head. His unbuttoned shirt opened to reveal a tantalising expanse of bronzed, muscular chest. This was the pose of the conqueror waiting for his concubine, and it thrilled her.

Aggie shrugged. 'They were free spirits. I liked it to start with. But I guess I'm not much of a free spirit.'

'No. You're not.' He gave her a slow, lingering smile that made her toes curl. 'Are you going to continue standing there or are you going to join me?' He patted the space next to him on the bed and Aggie's heart descended very rapidly in the direction of her feet.

She inched her way towards the bed and laughed when he sat forward and yanked her towards him. Her laughter felt like an unspoken release of all her defences. She was letting go of her resentment in the face of something bigger.

'What do you mean?' Heart beating a mile a minute, she collapsed next to him and felt the warmth of his body next to her. It generated a series of intensely physical reactions that left her breathless and gasping.

'So you're not impressed by money. But a free spirit would have taken what I offered— the computer, the extensive wardrobe; would have factored them in as gifts to be appreciated and moved on. You rejected the computer out of hand and agonised over the wardrobe. The only reason you accepted was because you had no more clothes and I had to talk you into seeing the sense behind the offer. And you still tell me you're going to return them all to me when we get back to London. You criticise me for wanting control but you fall victim to the very same tendency.'

'We're not alike at all.' They were both on their sides, fully clothed, staring at one another. There was something very erotic about the experience, because underneath the excitement of discovery lurked like a thrilling present concealed with wrapping paper.

'Money separates us,' Luiz said wryly. 'But in some areas I've discovered that we're remarkably similar. Would this conversation benefit from us being naked, do you think?'

Aggie released a small, treacherous moan and he delivered a rampantly satisfied smile in response. Then he stood up and held out one hand. 'I'm going to run a bath,' he murmured. 'Your room's next to mine. Why don't you go and get some clothes...?'

'It feels weird,' Aggie confided. 'I've never approached an intimate situation like this.'

'But then this is an intimate situation neither of us expected,' Luiz murmured. 'And that in itself is a first for me.'

'What do you mean?'

'It never fails to surprise me just how turned on I get for you.'

'Because I'm nothing like the women you've gone out with?'

'Because you're nothing like the women I've gone out with,' Luiz agreed.

Aggie knew that she should be offended by that, but then who would she be kidding? He was nothing like the guys she had gone out with. Mutual physical attraction had barrelled through everything and changed the parameters. Maybe that was why it felt so dangerously exciting.

'You're a lot more independent and I find that a turn on.' He softly ran his fingers along her side. He couldn't wait for her to be naked but this leisurely approach was intoxicating. 'You're not a slave to fashion and you're fond of arguing.'

Aggie conceded privately that all three of those things represented a change for him, but a change that he would rapidly tire of. Since she wasn't in it for the long haul, since she too was stepping outside the box, there was no harm in that, although she was uneasily aware of a barely acknowledged disappointment floating aimlessly inside her.

'You like your women submissive,' she said with a little laugh.

'Generally speaking, it's worked in the past.'

'And I like my guys to be creative, not to be ruled by money.'

'And yet, mysteriously, your creative paupers have all bitten the dust.' Luiz found, to his bemusement, that he didn't care for the thought of any other man in her life. It was puzzling, because he had never been the possessive type. In fact, in the past women who had tried to stir up a non-existent jealousy gene by referring to past lovers had succeeded in doing the opposite.

'They haven't been paupers,' Aggie laughed. 'Neither of them. They've just been indifferent to money.'

'And in the end they bored you.'

'I'm beginning to wish I'd never mentioned that,' Aggie said, though only half-joking. 'And if they bored me,' she felt obliged to elaborate, 'it was because they turned out to be boring people, not because they were indifferent to money.' She wriggled off the bed and stood up. 'Perhaps I'll have a bath in my own bathroom...'

Luiz frowned, propping himself up on one elbow. 'Second thoughts?' His voice was neutral but his eyes had cooled.

'No.' Aggie tilted her chin to look at him. 'I don't play games like that.'

'Good.' He felt himself relax. To have been rejected once bordered on the unthinkable. To be rejected twice would have been beyond the pale. 'Then what games do you play? Because I think I can help you out there...'

The promise behind those softly spoken words sent a shiver up her spine and it was still there when she returned to his bedroom a few minutes later. She had not been lying when she had confessed that she had never approached sex like this before. Stripped of all romantic mystique and airy-fairy expectations that it would lead somewhere, this was physical contact reduced to its most concentrated form.

The bath had been run. Aggie could smell the fragrance of jasmine bath oil. The steam in the enormous bathroom did nothing whatsoever to diminish the impact of Luiz, who had stripped out of his clothes and was wearing a towel around his waist.

Outside, the snow continued to fall. In her room, she had taken a few seconds to stare out of the window and absorb the fact that Mark and Maria, and the mission upon which they had embarked only a few days previously, couldn't have been further from her mind. When exactly had she lost track of the reason why she was here in the first place? It was as though she had opened the wardrobe door to find herself stepping into Narnia, reality left behind for a brief window in time.

She could barely remember the routine of her day-to-day existence. The school, the staff room, the kids getting ready for their Nativity play.

Was Luiz right? She had always fancied herself as a free-spirited person and yet she felt as though this was the first impulsive thing she had ever done in her life. She had thought him freakishly controlled, a power-hungry tycoon addicted to mastering everything and everyone around him, while she—well, she was completely different. Maybe the only difference really was the fact that he was rich and she wasn't, that he had grown up with privilege while she had had to fight her way out of her background, burying herself in studies that could provide her with opportunities.

'Now, what I'd like...' Luiz drawled, and Aggie blinked herself back to the present, 'is to do what I was fantasising about when you did your little catwalk in that shop for me. Instead of showing me how you look with clothes on, show me how you look with them off.'

He sauntered out of the bathroom and lay back down on the bed, just as he had before.

Aggie realised in some part of her that, whilst this should not feel right, it did. She would never have believed it possible for either of them to set aside their personal differences and meet on this plane. Certainly, she would never have believed it of herself, but before she could begin nurturing any doubts about the radical decision she had made she told herself that everyone deserves some time out, and this was her time out. In a day or two, it would be nothing more than a wicked memory of the one and only time she had truly strayed from the path she had laid out for herself.

She watched, fascinated and tingling all over, shocked as he drew back the towel which had been modestly covering him, and revealed his arousal. She nearly fainted when he gently held it in one hand.

Luiz grinned at her. 'So easy to make you blush,' he murmured. Then he fell silent and watched as she began removing her clothes, at first with self-conscious, fumbling fingers, then with more confidence as she revelled in the sight of his darkened, openly appreciative gaze.

'Come here,' he rasped roughly, before she could remove the final strips of clothing. 'I'm finding it hard to wait.'

Aggie sighed and flung her head back as his big hands curved over her breasts, thinly sheathed in a lacy bra. Their mouths met in an explosive kiss, a greedy, hungry kiss, so that they gasped as they surfaced for air and then resumed their kissing as if neither could get enough of the other. Her nipples were tender and sensitive and she moaned when he rolled his thumb over one stiffened peak, seeking and finding it through the lacy gaps in the bra.

She was melting. Freeing a hand from the tangle of his black hair, she shakily pulled off the panties which were damp, proof of her own out-of-control libido.

Luiz was going crazy with *wanting* her. He could hardly bear the brief separation of their bodies as she unclasped her bra from the back and pulled it off.

Her nipples were big, circular discs, clearly defined, pouting temptingly at him. He realised that he had been fantasising about this moment perhaps from the very first time he had laid eyes on her. He had not allowed himself to see her in a sexual way, not when he had been busy working out how to disengage her and her brother from his niece and the family fortune. But enforced time together had whittled away his self-control. It had allowed the seeds of attraction to take root and flourish.

'You have the face of an angel,' he breathed huskily as he rolled her on top of him. 'And the body of a siren.'

'I'm not sure about that.' Aggie gazed down at him. 'Aren't sirens supposed to be voluptuous?'

'God, you're beautiful...' His hands could almost span her waist and he eased her down so that he could take one of those delicate breasts to his mouth and suckle on the hot, throbbing tip. He loved the way she arched her body back, offering herself to him—and even more he loved the way he could sense her spiralling out of control, her fists clenched as she tried to control the waves of sensation washing over her.

He smoothed his hand along the inside of her thigh and she wriggled to accommodate his questing finger. She shuddered when that finger dipped into her honeyed moistness and began stroking her. With her body under sensual attack on two fronts as he continued to worship her breast with his mouth and tease the wet, receptive bud of her femininity with his finger, she could bear it no longer. She flipped off him and lay on her back, breathing heavily and then curling onto her side as he laughed softly next to her.

'Too much?' he asked, and she sighed on a moan.

'Not fair. It's your turn now to feel like you're about to fall off the edge.'

'What makes you think I'm not already there?'

It transpired that he wasn't. In fact, it transpired that he didn't have a clue what being close to the edge was all about. He had foolishly been confusing it with simply *being turned on*.

For an excruciatingly long period of time, she demonstrated what being close to the edge was all about. She touched him and tasted him until he thought he had died and gone to heaven.

Their bodies seemed to merge and become one. She touched him and he touched her, from her breasts, down to her flat belly with its little mole just above her belly button, and then at last to the most intimate part of her.

He peeled apart her delicate folds and dipped his tongue just there until she squirmed with pleasure, her fingers tangled in his hair, her eyes shut and her whole body thrust back to receive the ministrations of his mouth.

He lazily feasted on her silky-sweet moistness until she was begging him to stop. Lost in the moment, he could have stayed there for ever with her legs around him and her body bucking under his mouth.

He finally thrust into her only after he was wearing protection. Putting it on, he found that his hands were shaking. He kicked off the last slither of duvet that remained on the bed and she opened up to him like a flower, her rhythm and movements matching his so that they were moving as one.

Aggie didn't think that she had ever felt so united and in tune with another human being in her life before. Her body was slippery, coated in a fine film of perspiration. His was too.

They climaxed and it was like soaring high above the earth. And then, quietening, they subsided gently back down. She rolled onto her side and looked at him with pleasure.

'That was...'

'Momentous? Beyond description?' God, this was nothing like what he had felt before! Could good sex do this to a man? Make him feel like he could fly? They had only just finished making love and he couldn't wait to take her again. Did that make sense? He had made love to any number of beautiful women before but he had never felt like this. He had never felt as though he was in possession of an insatiable appetite, had never wanted to switch the light on so that he could just *look*...

'I want to take you again, but first...' Luiz felt an urgent need to set a few facts straight, to reassure himself that this feeling of being out of control, carried away by a current against which he seemed to be powerless, was just a temporary situation. 'You know this isn't going to go anywhere, don't you?' He brushed her hair away from her face so that he could look her directly in the eye. So this might be the wrong time and the wrong place to say this, but it had to be said. He had to clear the air. 'I wouldn't want you to think...'

'Shh. I don't think anything.' Aggie smiled bravely while a series of pathways began connecting in her brain. This man she loathed, to whom she was desperately attracted, was a man who could make her laugh even though she had found him overbearing and arrogant, the same man who had slowly filled her head and her heart. It was why she was here now. In bed with him. She hadn't suddenly become a woman with no morals who thought it was fine to jump into bed on the basis of sexual attraction. No. That had been a little piece of fiction she had sold herself because the truth staring her in the face had been unacceptable.

'I'm not about to start making demands. You

and I, we're not suited and we never will be. But we're attracted to one another. That's all. So, why don't we just have some fun? Because we both know that tomorrow it all comes to an end.'

CHAPTER EIGHT

AGGIE spent the night in her own bedroom. Drunk with love-making, she had made sure to tiptoe along the corridor at a little after two in the morning. It was important to remind herself that this was not a normal relationship. It had boundaries and Luiz had made sure to remind her of that the night before. She wasn't about to over step any of them.

She heard the beeping of her phone the following morning and woke to find a series of messages from her brother, all asking her to give him a call.

Panicked, Aggie sat up and dialled his mobile with shaking fingers. She was ashamed to admit that her brother had barely registered on her radar over the past few hours. In fact, she guiltily realised that she had been too focused on herself for longer than that to spare much thought for Mark.

She got through to him almost immediately.

The conversation, on her end, barely covered a sentence or two. Down the other end of the line, Mark did all the talking and at the end of ten minutes Aggie ended the call, shell-shocked.

Everything was about to change now, and for a few seconds she resented her brother's intrusion into the little bubble she had built for herself. She checked the time on her phone. Luiz had tried to pull her back into bed with him before she had left in the early hours of the morning, but Aggie had resisted. Luiz was a man who always got what he wanted and rarely paused to consider the costs. He wanted her and would see nothing wrong in having her, whenever and wherever. He was good when it came to detaching and, once their time together was over, he would instantly break off and walk away. Aggie knew that she would not be able to, so putting some distance between them, if not sharing a room for the night could be termed putting distance between them, was essential.

So they had agreed to meet for breakfast at nine. Plenty of time to check the weather and for Luiz to catch up with emails. It was now a little after eight, and Aggie was glad for the time in which she could have a bath and think about what her brother had told her.

Luiz was waiting for her in the dining room, where a pot of coffee was already on the table and two menus, one of which he was scanning, although he put it down as she hovered for a few seconds in the doorway.

She was in a pair of faded jeans and a blue jumper, her hair tied back. She looked like a very sexy schoolgirl, and all at once he felt himself stir into lusty arousal. He hadn't been able to get enough of her the night before. In fact, he recalled asking her at one point whether she was too sore for him to touch her again down there. He leaned back in the chair and shot her a sexy half-smile as she walked towards him.

'You should have stayed with me,' were his first words of greeting. 'You would have made an unbeatable wake-up call.'

Aggie slipped into the chair opposite and helped herself to some coffee. Mark and his news were at the top of her mind but it was something she would lead up to carefully.

'You said you wanted to get some work done

before you came down to breakfast. I wouldn't have wanted to interrupt you.'

'I'm good at multi-tasking. You'd be surprised how much work I can get through when there's someone between my legs paying attention to…'

'Shh!' She went bright red and Luiz laughed, entertained at her prurience.

'You get my drift, though?'

'Is that the kind of wake-up call you're accustomed to?' She held the cup between her hands and looked at him over the rim. She had kept her voice light but underneath she could feel jealousy swirling through her veins, unwelcome and inappropriate.

'The only wake-up calls I'm accustomed to are the ones that come from alarm clocks.' He hadn't thought about it, but women sleeping in his bed didn't happen.

'You mean you've never had a night with a woman in your bed? What about holidays?'

'I don't do holidays with women.'

Aggie gazed at him in surprise.

'It's not that unusual,' Luiz muttered, shooting her a brooding look from under his lashes. 'I'm a busy man. I don't have time for the demands of a woman on holiday.'

'How on earth do you ever relax?'

'I return to Brazil. My holidays are there.' He shrugged. 'I used to go on holidays with a couple of my pals. The occasional weekend. Usually skiing. Those have dried up over the past few years.'

'Your holidays were with your guy friends?'

'How did we end up having this conversation?' He raked his fingers through his dark hair in a gesture that she had come to recognise as one of frustration.

If this was about sex and nothing more—and he had made it clear that for him it was—then Aggie knew she should steer clear of in-depth conversations. He wouldn't welcome them. She fancied that it had always been his way of avoiding the commitment of a full-blown relationship, his way of keeping women at a safe distance. If you didn't have any kind of revealing conversation with someone, then it was unlikely that anyone would ever get close to you. Her curiosity felt like a treacherous step in dangerous waters.

'There's nothing wrong with talking to one another.' She glanced down at the menu and made noises about scrambled eggs and toast.

'Guys don't need attention to be lavished on them,' Luiz said abruptly. 'We're all experienced skiers. We do the black runs, relax for a couple of hours in the evening. Good exercise. No one complaining about not being entertained.'

'I can't imagine anyone having the nerve to complain to you,' Aggie remarked, and Luiz relaxed.

'You'd be surprised, although women complaining fades into insignificance when set alongside your remarkable talent for arguing with me. Not that I don't like it. It's your passionate nature. Your *extremely* passionate nature.'

'Plus those chalet girls can be very attractive if you decide you miss the entertainment of females...'

Luiz laughed, his dark eyes roaming appreciatively over her face. 'When I go skiing, I ski. The last thing I've ever wanted is any kind of involvement in those brief windows of leisure time I get round to snatching for myself.'

'And those brief windows have dried up?'

'My father hasn't been well,' Luiz heard himself say. It was a surprising admission and not one he could remember making to anyone. Only he and his mother knew the real state of his father's health. Like him, his father didn't appreciate fuss and he knew that his daughters would fuss around him. He was also the primary figurehead for the family's vast empire. Many of the older clients would react badly to any hint that Alfredo Montes was not in the prime of good health. Whilst for years Luiz had concentrated on his own business concerns, he had been obliged to take a much more active role in his father's various companies over the past few years, slowly building confidence for the day when his father could fully retire.

'I'm sorry.' She reached out and covered his hand with hers. 'What's wrong with him?'

'Forget I said anything.'

'Why? Is it…terminal?'

Luiz hesitated. 'He had a stroke a few years ago and never made a full recovery. He can still function, but not in the way he used to. His memory isn't what it used to be, nor are his levels of concentration. He's been forced into semi-retirement.

No one is aware of his health issues aside from me and my mother.'

'So...you've been overseeing his affairs so that he can slow down?'

'It's not a big deal.' He beckoned across a waitress, closing down the conversation while Aggie fitted that background information about him into the bigger picture she was unconsciously building.

Luiz Montes was a workaholic who had found himself in a situation where he couldn't afford to stand still. He had no time for holidays and even less for the clutter of a relationship. But, even into that relentless lifestyle, he had managed to fit in this tortuous trip on behalf of his sister. It proclaimed family loyalty and a generosity of spirit that she had not given him credit for.

'There's something you need to know,' she said, changing the subject. 'Mark finally got through to me this morning. In fact, last night. I left my phone in the bedroom and didn't check it before I went to sleep. I woke up this morning to find missed calls and text messages for me to call him.'

'And?'

'They're not in the Lake District after all. They're in Las Vegas.'

'So they did it. They tied the knot, the bloody fools.' Luiz didn't feel the rage he had expected. He was still dwelling on the uncustomary lapse in judgement that had allowed him to confide in her. He had never felt the need to pour his heart and soul out to anyone. Indeed, he had always viewed such tendencies as weaknesses, but strangely sharing that secret had had a liberating effect. Enough to smooth over any anger he knew he should have been feeling at his niece doing something as stupid as getting married when she was still a child herself.

'I never said that.' Aggie grinned and he raised his eyebrows enquiringly.

'Share the joke? Because I'm not seeing anything funny from where I'm sitting.' But he could feel himself just going through the motions.

'Well, for a start, they haven't got married.'

Luiz looked at her in silence. 'Come again?'

'Your sister was obviously worried for no good reason. Okay, maybe Maria confided that she loved my brother. Maybe she indulged in a bit of girlish wishful thinking, but that was as far as it went. There was never any plan to run away and get married in the dead of night.'

'So we've spent the past few days on a fool's errand? What the hell are they doing in *Las Vegas*?' Less than a week ago, he would have made a sarcastic comment about the funding for such a trip, but then less than a week ago he hadn't been marooned with this woman in the middle of nowhere. Right at this moment in time, he really couldn't give a damn who had paid for what or who was ripping whom off.

He found himself thinking of that foster home—the atmosphere of cheeriness despite the old furnishings and the obvious lack of luxuries. He thought of Aggie's dingy rented house. Both those things should have hit him as evidence of people not out to take what they could get.

'Mark's over the moon.' Aggie rested her chin in the palm of her hand and looked at Luiz with shining eyes. 'He got a call when they'd only just left London. He said that he was going to call me but then he knew that he wasn't expected back for a few days and he didn't want to say anything just in case nothing came of it. But through a friend of a friend of a friend, a record producer got to hear one of his demos and flew them both over so that they could hear some more. He's got a recording contract!'

'Well, I'll be damned.'

'So...' Aggie sat back to allow a plate of eggs and toast to be put in front of her. 'There's no point carrying on any further.'

'No, there isn't.'

'You'll be relieved, I bet. You can get back to your work, although I'm going to preach at you now and tell you that it's not healthy to work the hours you do, even if you feel you have no choice.'

'You're probably right.'

'I mean, you need to be able to enjoy leisure time as much as you enjoy working time. Sorry? What did you say?'

Luiz shrugged. 'When we get back to London.' He hadn't intended on having any kind of relationship with her, but after last night he couldn't foresee relinquishing it just yet. 'A slight reduction in the workload wouldn't hurt. It's the Christmas season. People are kicking back. It's not as frenetic in the business world as it usually is.'

'So you're going to take a holiday?' Aggie's

heart did a sudden, painful flip. 'Will you be going to Brazil, then?'

'I can't leave the country just yet.'

'I thought you said that you were going to have a break.'

'Which isn't to say that I'm suddenly going to drop out of sight. There are a couple of deals that need work, meetings I can't get out of.' He pushed his plate away and sat back to look at her steadily. 'We need to talk about…us. This.'

'I know. It wasn't the wisest move in the world. Neither of us anticipated that…that…'

'That we wouldn't be able to keep our hands off one another?'

How easy it was for him to think about it purely in terms of sex, Aggie thought. While *she* could only think of it in terms of falling in love. She wondered how many women before her had made the same mistake of bucking the guidelines he set and falling in love with him. Had his last girl friend been guilty of that sin?

'The circumstances were peculiar,' Aggie said, keen to be as light-hearted about what happened between them as he was. 'It's a fact that people can behave out of character when they're thrown into a situation they're not accustomed to. I mean, none of this would have happened if we hadn't... found ourselves snowbound on this trip.'

'Wouldn't it?' His dark eyes swept thoughtfully over her flushed face.

'What do you mean?'

'I like to think I'm honest enough not to under-estimate this attraction I feel for you. I noticed you the first time I saw you and it wasn't just as a potential gold-digger. I think I was sexually attracted to you from the beginning. Maybe I would never have done anything about it but I wouldn't bet on that.'

'*I* didn't notice you!'

'Liar.'

'I didn't,' Aggie insisted with a touch of des-peration. 'I mean, I just thought you were Maria's arrogant uncle who had only appeared on the scene to warn us off. I didn't even like you!'

'Who's talking about like or dislike? That's quite different from sexual attraction. Which brings me back to my starting point. We'll head back down to London as soon as we've finished breakfast, and when we get to London I want to know what your plans are. Because I'm not ready to give this up just yet. In fact, I would say that I'm just getting started...'

Just yet. Didn't that say it all? But at least he wasn't trying to disguise the full extent of his interest in her; at least he wasn't pretending that they were anything but two ships passing in the night, dropping anchor for a while before moving on their separate journeys.

When Aggie thought of her last boyfriend, he had been fond of planning ahead, discussing where they would go on holiday in five years' time. She had fancied herself in love, but like an illness it had passed quickly and soon after she had realised that what she had really loved was the feeling of permanence that had been promised.

Luiz wasn't promising permanence. In fact, he wasn't even promising anything longer than a couple of weeks or a couple of months.

'You're looking for another notch on your bedpost?' Aggie said lightly and he frowned at her.

'I'm not that kind of man and if you don't think I've been honest with you, then I can only repeat what I've said. I'm not looking for a committed relationship, but neither do I work my way through women because I have a little black book I want to fill. If you really think that, then we're not on the same page, and whatever we did last night will remain a one-time memory.'

'I shouldn't have said that, but Luiz, you can't really blame me, can you? I mean, have you ever had a relationship that you thought might be going somewhere?'

'I've never sought it. On the other hand, I don't use women. Why are we discussing this, Aggie? Neither of us sees any kind of future in this. I thought we'd covered that.' He looked at her narrowly. 'We *have* covered that, haven't we? I mean, you haven't suddenly decided that you're looking for a long-term relationship, have you? Because, I repeat, it's never going to happen.'

'I'm aware of that,' Aggie snapped. 'And, believe me, I'm not on the hunt for anything permanent either.'

'Then what's the problem? Why the sudden atmosphere?' He allowed a few seconds of thoughtful silence during which time she tried to think of something suitably dismissive to say. 'I never asked,' he said slowly. 'But I assumed that when you slept with me there was no one else in your life…'

Aggie's blue eyes were wide with confusion as she returned his gaze, then comprehension filtered through and confusion turned to anger.

'That's a horrible thing to say.' She felt tears prick the back of her eyes and she hurriedly stared down at her plate.

Luiz shook his head, shame-faced and yet wanting to tell her that, horrible it might be, but it wouldn't be the first time a woman had slept with him while still involved with another man. Some women enjoyed hedging their bets. Naturally, once he was involved, all other men were instantly dropped, but from instances like that he had developed a healthy dose of suspicion when it came to the opposite sex.

But, hell, he couldn't lump Aggie into the same category as other women. She was in a league of her own.

Cheeks flushed, Aggie flung down her napkin and stood up. 'If we're leaving, I need to go upstairs and get my packing done.'

'Aggie…' Luiz vaulted to his feet and followed her as she stormed out of the dining room to wards the staircase. He grabbed her by her arm and pulled her towards him.

'It doesn't matter.'

'It *matters*. I…I apologise for what I said.'

'You're so suspicious of everyone! What kind of world do you live in, Luiz Montes? You're suspicious of gold-diggers, opportunists, women who want to take advantage of you…'

'It's ingrained, and I'm not saying that it's a good thing.' But it was something he had never questioned before. He looked at her, confused, frowning. 'I want to carry on seeing you when we get back to London,' he said roughly.

'And you've laid down so many guidelines about what that entails!' Aggie sighed and shook her head. This was so bad for her, yet even while one part of her brain acknowledged that there was another part that couldn't contemplate giving him up without a backward glance. Even standing this close to him was already doing things to her, making her heart beat faster and turning her bones to jelly.

'I'm just attempting to be as honest as I can.'

'And you don't have to worry that I'm going to do anything stupid!' She looked at him fiercely.

If only he knew how stupid she had already been he would run a mile. But, just as she had jumped in feet first to sleep with him and damn the consequences, she was going to carry on sleeping with him, taking what she could get like an addict too scared of quitting until it was forced upon them.

She wasn't proud of herself but, like him, she was honest.

Luiz half-closed his eyes with relief. He only realised that he had been holding his breath when he expelled it slowly. 'The drive back will be a lot easier,' he said briskly. His hand on her arm turned to a soft caress that sent shivers racing up and down her spine.

'And are you still going to...talk to Mark when they get back from London? Warn him of Maria?'

Luiz realised that he hadn't given that any thought at all. 'They're not getting married. Crisis defused.' He looked at her and grinned reluctantly. 'Okay. I've had other things on my mind I hadn't given any thought to what was going to happen next in this little saga. Now I'm thinking about it and realising that Luisa can have whatever mother-to-daughter chat she thinks she needs to have. I'm removing myself from the situation.'

'I'm glad.'

She smiled and all Luiz could think was that he was chuffed that he had been responsible for putting that smile on her face.

Once, he would not have been able to see beyond the fact that any relationship where the levels of wealth were so disproportionately unbalanced was doomed to failure, if not worse. Once the financial inequality would have been enough for him to continue his pursuit, to do everything within his power to remove Aggie's brother from any position from which he could exert influence over his niece. Things had subtly changed.

'So,' she said softly. 'I'm going to go and pack and I'll see you back here in half an hour or so?'

Luiz nodded and she didn't ask for any details of what would happen next. Of course, they would return to her house, but then what? Would they date one another or was that too romantic a notion for him? Would he wine and dine her, the way he wined and dined the other women he went out with? She was sure that he was generous when it came to the materialistic side of any relationship he was in. What he lacked in emotional giving, he would more than make up for in financial generosity. He was, after all, the man who had suggested buying her a laptop computer because she happened not to possess one. And this before they had become lovers.

But, if he had his ground rules, then she had hers. She would not allow him to buy anything for her nor would she expect any lavish meals out or expensive seats at the opera or the theatre. If his approach to what they had was to put all his cards on the table, then she would have to make sure that she put some of her own cards on the table as well.

As if predicating for a quick journey back to London, as opposed to the tortuous one they had embarked upon when they had set off, the snow had finally dwindled to no more than some soft light flurries.

The atmosphere was heavy with the thrill of what lay ahead. Aggie was conscious of every movement of his hands on the steering wheel. She sneaked glances at his profile and marvelled at the sexy perfection of his face. When she closed her eyes, she imagined being alone with him in a room, submitting to his caresses.

Making small talk just felt like part of an elaborate dance between them. He was planning on visiting his family in Brazil over the Christmas period. She asked him about where he lived. She found that she had an insatiable appetite for finding out all the details of his background. Having broken ground with his confidences about his father, he talked about him, about the stroke and the effect it had had on him. He described his country in ways that brought it alive. She felt as though there were a million things she wanted to hear about him.

Mark and Maria would not be returning to the country for a few days yet, and as they approached the outskirts of London he said in a lazy drawl that already expected agreement to his proposal, 'I don't think you should carry on living in that dump.'

Aggie laughed, amused.

'I'm not kidding. I can't have you living there.'

'Where would you have me living, Luiz?'

'Kensington has some decent property. I could get you somewhere.'

'Thanks, but I think we've already covered the problem of rent in London and how expensive it is.'

'You misunderstand me. When I say that I could get you somewhere, I mean I could *buy* you somewhere.'

Aggie's mouth dropped open and she looked at him in astonishment and disbelief.

'Well?' Luiz prompted, when there was silence following this remark.

'You can't just go and *buy somewhere* for a woman you happen to be sleeping with, Luiz.'

'Why not?'

'Because it's not right.'

'I want you to live somewhere halfway decent. I have the money to turn that wish into reality. What could be more right?'

'And just for the sake of argument, what would happen with this halfway decent house when we broke up?'

Luiz frowned, not liking the way that sounded. He knew he was the one who'd laid down that rule, but was there really any need to underline it and stick three exclamation marks after it for good measure?

'You'd keep it, naturally. I never give a woman gifts and then take them away from her when the relationship goes sour.'

'You've had way too much your own way for too long,' Aggie told him. It was hardly surprising. He had grown up with money and it had always been second nature to indulge his women with gifts. 'I'm not going to accept a house from you. Or a flat, or whatever. I'm perfectly happy where I am.'

'You're not,' Luiz contradicted bluntly. 'No one could be perfectly happy in that hovel. The closest anyone could get to feeling anything about that place is that it's a roof over your head.'

'I don't want anything from you.' After the great open spaces of up north, the business of London felt like four walls pressing down on her.

That was not what Luiz wanted to hear, because for once he *wanted* to give her things. He wanted to see that smile on her face and know that he was responsible for putting it there.

'Actually,' Aggie continued thoughtfully, 'I think we should just enjoy whatever we have. I don't want you giving me any presents or taking me to expensive places.'

'I don't do home-cooked meals in front of the television.'

'And I don't do lavish meals out. Now and again, it's nice to go somewhere for dinner, but it's nice not to as well.' Aggie knew that she was treading on thin ice here. Any threat of domesticity would have him running a mile, but how much should she sacrifice for the sake of love and lust?

'I'm not into all that stuff,' she said. 'I don't wear jewels and I don't have expensive tastes.'

'Why are you so difficult?'

'I didn't realise I was.'

'From a practical point of view, your house is going to be a little cramped with your brother there and my niece popping her head in every three minutes. I'm not spending time at your place with the four of us sitting on a sagging sofa, watching television while my car gets broken into outside.'

Aggie laughed aloud. 'That's a very weak argument for getting your own way.'

'Well, you can't blame a guy for trying.'

But he wished to God he had tried a little harder when they finally arrived back at her dismal house in west London. Snow had turned to slush and seemed to have infused the area with a layer of unappealing grey.

Aggie looked at him as he reviewed the house with an expression of thinly concealed disgust and she smiled. He was so spoiled, so used to getting everything he wanted. It was true that he had not complained once at any of the discomforts he had had to endure on their little trip, at least at any of the things which in his rarefied world would have counted as discomforts. But it would be getting on his nerves that he couldn't sort this one out. Especially when he had a point. Mr Cholmsey couldn't have created a less appealing abode to rent if he had tried.

She wondered how she could have forgotten the state of disrepair it was in.

'You could at least come back with me to my apartment,' Luiz said, lounging against the wall in the hallway as Aggie dumped her bag on the ground. 'Indulge yourself, Aggie.' His voice was as smooth as chocolate and as tempting. 'There's nothing wrong with wanting to relax in a place where the central heating doesn't sound like a car backfiring every two minutes.'

Aggie looked helplessly at him, caught up in a moment of indecision. He bent to kiss her, a sweet, delicate kiss as he tasted her mouth, not touching her anywhere else, in fact hardly moving from his indolent pose against the wall.

'Not fair,' she murmured.

'I want to get you into my bath,' Luiz murmured softly. 'My very big, very clean bath, a bath that can easily fit the both of us. And then afterwards I want you in my bed, my extra-wide and extra-long king-sized bed with clean linen. And if you're really intent on us doing the telly thing, you can switch on the television in my bedroom; it's as big as a cinema screen. But before that, I want to make love to you in comfort, and then when we're both spent I want to send out for a meal from my guy at the Savoy. No need for you to dress up or go out, just the two of us. He does an excellent chocolate mousse for dessert. I'd really like to have it flavoured with a bit of you...'

'You win,' Aggie said on a sigh of pure pleasure. She reached up and pulled him down to her and in the end they found themselves clinging to one another as they wended an unsteady path up to her bedroom.

Despite Luiz's adamant proclamations that he wanted to have her in his house, she was so damned delectable that he couldn't resist.

Her top was off by the time they hit the top of the stairs. By the bedroom door, her bra was draped over the banister and she had wriggled out of her jeans just as they both collapsed onto the bed which, far from being king-sized, was only slightly bigger than a single.

'I've been wanting to do this from the second we got into my car to drive back to London,' Luiz growled, in a manner that was decidedly un-cool. 'In fact, I was very tempted to book us into a room in the first hotel we came to just so that I could do this. I don't know what it is about you, but the second I'm near you I turn into a caveman.'

Aggie decided that she liked the sound of that. She lay back and watched as he rid himself of his clothes. This was frantic sex, two slippery bodies entwined. Leisurely foreplay would have to wait, he told her, he just needed to feel himself inside her, hot and wet and waiting for him.

Luiz could say things that drove her wild, and he drove her wild now as he huskily told her just how she made him feel when they were having sex.

Every graphic description made her wetter and more turned on and when he entered her she was so close to the edge that she had to grit her teeth together to hold herself back.

His movements were deep, his shaft big and powerful, taking her higher and higher until she cried out as she climaxed. Her nails dug into his shoulder blades and she arched back, her head tilted back, her eyes closed, her nostrils slightly flared.

She was the most beautiful creature Luiz had ever laid eyes on. He felt himself explode inside her and by then it was too late. He couldn't hold it back. He certainly couldn't retrieve the results of his ferocious orgasm and he collapsed next to her with a groan.

'I didn't use protection.' He was still coming down from a high but his voice was harshly self admonishing, bitterly angry for his oversight. He looked at her, then sat up, legs over the side of the bed, head in his hands, and cursed silently under his breath.

'It's okay,' Aggie said quickly. Well, if she hadn't got the message that this was a man who didn't want to settle down, then she was getting it now loud and clear. Not only did he not want to settle down, but the mere thought of a pregnancy was enough to turn him white with horror.

'I'm safe.'

Luiz exhaled with relief and lay back down next to her. 'Hell, I've never made that mistake in my life before. I don't know what happened.' But he did. He had lost control. This was not the man he was. He didn't lose control.

Looking at him, Aggie could see the disgust on his face that he could ever have been stupid enough, *human* enough to make a slip-up.

For all the ways he could get under her skin, she reminded herself that Luiz Montes was not available for anything other than a casual affair. She might love him but she should look for nothing more than unrequited love.

CHAPTER NINE

'WHAT's wrong?' Luiz looked at Aggie across the width of the table in the small chain restauran where he had just been subjected to a distinctly mediocre pizza and some even more mediocre wine.

'Nothing's wrong.' But Aggie couldn't meet hi eyes. He had a way of looking at her. It made he feel as though he could see down to the bottom of her soul, as though he could dredge up thing she wanted to keep to herself.

The past month had been the most amazing time of her life. She had had the last week a school, where the snow had lingered for a few days until finally all that had been left were the remains of two snowmen which the children had built.

Luiz had visited her twice at school. The firs time he had just shown up. All the other teach ers had been agog. The children had stared

Aggie had felt embarrassed, but embarrassed in a proud way. Everyone, all her friends at the school, would be wondering how she had managed to grab the attention of someone like Luiz, even if they didn't come right out and say it. And, frankly, Aggie still wondered how she had managed to achieve that. She didn't think that she could ever fail to get a kick just looking at him and when those dark, fabulous eyes rested on her she didn't think that she could ever fail to melt.

He had returned to Brazil for a few days over Christmas. Aggie had decided that it would be a good time to get her act together and use his absence to start building a protective shell around her, but the very second she had seen him again she had fallen straight back into the bottomless hole from which she had intended to start climbing out.

She felt as though she was on a rollercoaster. Her whole system was fired up when he was around and there wasn't a single second when she didn't want to be in his company, although at the back of her mind she knew that the rollercoaster ride would end and when it did she would be left dazed and shaken and turned inside out.

'It's this place!' Luiz flung his napkin on his half-eaten pizza and sat back in his chair.

'What?'

'Why are you too proud to accept my invitations to restaurants where the food is at least edible?'

Aggie looked at him, momentarily distracted by the brooding sulkiness on his dark face. He looked ridiculously out of place here. So tall, striking and exotic, surrounded by families with chattering kids and teenagers. But she hadn't wanted to go anywhere intimate with him. She had wanted somewhere bright, loud and impersonal.

'You've taken me to loads of expensive restaurants,' she reminded him. 'I could start listing them if you'd like.'

Luiz waved his hand dismissively. Something was wrong and he didn't like it. He had grown accustomed to her effervescence, to her teasing, to the way she made him feel as though the only satisfactory end to his day was when he saw her. Right now she was subdued, her bright-blue eyes clouded, and he didn't like the fact that he couldn't reach her.

'We need to get the bill and clear out of here,' he growled, signalling to a waitress, who appeared so quickly that Aggie thought she might have been hanging around waiting for him to call her across. 'I can think of better things to do than sit here with cold, congealing food on our plates, waiting for our tempers to deteriorate.'

'No!'

'What do you mean, *no?*' Luiz narrowed his eyes on her flushed face. Her gaze skittered away and she licked her lips nervously. The thought of her not wanting to head back to his place as fast as they could suddenly filled him with a sense of cold dread.

'I mean, it's still early.' Aggie dragged the sentence out while she frantically tried to think of how she would say what she had to say. 'Plus it's Saturday. Everyone's out having fun.'

'Well, let's go have some fun somewhere else.' He leaned towards her and shot her a wolfish grin. 'Making love doesn't have to be confined to a bedroom. A change of scenery would work for me too…'

'A change of scenery?' Aggie asked faintly. She giddily lost herself in his persuasive, sexy, slow smile. He had come directly to her house, straight from the office, and he was still in his work clothes: a dark grey, hand-tailored suit. The tie would be bunched up in the pocket of his jacket, which he had slung over the back of the chair along with his coat, and he had rolled up the sleeves of his shirt. He looked every inch the billionaire businessman and once again she was swept away on an incredulous wave of not knowing how he could possibly be attracted to her.

And yet there were times, and lots of them, when they seemed like two halves of the same coin. Aggie had grown fond of recalling those times. Half of her knew that it was just wishful thinking on her part, a burning desire to see him relating to her in more than just an insatiably sexual capacity, but there was no harm in dreaming, was there?

'I'm losing you again.' Luiz ran his fingers through his hair and looked at her with an impatient shake of his head. 'Come on. We're getting out of here. I've had enough of this cheap and cheerful family eaterie. There's more to a Saturday night than this.'

He stood up and waited as she scrambled to her

feet. It was still cold outside, but without the bite of before Christmas, when it had hurt just being outdoors. Aggie knew she should have stayed put inside the warm, noisy, crowded restaurant but coward that she was, she wanted to leave as much as he did.

Once she would have been more than satisfied with a meal out at the local pizzeria but now she could see that it could hardly be called a dining experience. It was a place to grab something or to bring kids where they could make as much mess as they wanted without staff getting annoyed.

'We could go back to my house,' Aggie said reluctantly as Luiz swung his arm over her shoulders and reached out to hail a cab with the other.

He touched her as though it was the most natural thing in the world. It was just something else she had relegated to her wishful-thinking cupboard. *If he can be so relaxed with me, surely there's more to what we have than sex...?*

Except not once had he ever hinted at what that something else might be. He never spoke of future and she knew that he was careful not to give her any ideas. He had warned her at the beginning of their relationship that he wasn't into permanence and he had assumed that the warning held good.

He didn't love her. She was a temporary part of his life and he enjoyed her and she had given him no indication that it was any different for her.

'And where's your brother?'

'He might be there with Maria. I don't know. As you know, he leaves for America on Monday. I think he was planning on cooking something special for them.'

'So your suggestion is we return to that dump where we'll be fighting for space alongside your brother and my niece, interrupting their final, presumably romantic meal together. Unless, of course, we hurry up to your unheated bedroom where we can squash into your tiny bed and make love as noiselessly as possible.'

Luiz loathed her house but he had given up trying to persuade her to move out to something bigger, more comfortable and paid for by him. She had dug her heels in and refused to budge, but the upshot was that they spent very little time there. In fact, the more Aggie saw her house through his eyes, the more dissatisfied she was with it.

'There's no need to be difficult!' Aggi

snapped, pulling away to stare up at him. 'Why do you always have to get your own way?'

'If I always got my own way then explain why we've just spent an hour and a half in a place where the food is average and the noise levels are high enough to give people migraines. What the hell is going on, Aggie? I didn't meet you so that I could battle my way through a bad mood!'

'I can't always be sunshine and light, Luiz!'

They stared at each other. Aggie was hardly aware of the approach of a black cab until she was being hustled into it. She heard Luiz curtly give his address and sighed with frustration, because the last place she wanted to be with him was at his apartment.

'Now...' He turned to face her and extended his arm along the back of the seat. 'Talk to me. Tell me what's going on.' His eyes drifted to the mutinous set of her mouth and he wanted to do nothing more than kiss it back into smiling submission. He wasn't normally given to issuing invitations to women to talk. He was a man of action and his preferred choice, when faced with a woman who clearly *wanted to talk*, was to bury all chat between the sheets. But Aggie, he had to

concede, was different. If he suggested buryin
the chat between the sheets, she would probabl
round on him with the full force of her feisty
outspoken, brazenly argumentative personality

'We do need to talk,' she admitted quietly, an
she felt him go still next to her.

'Well, I'm all ears.'

'Not here. We might as well wait till we get t
your place, although I would have preferred t
have this conversation in the restaurant.'

'You mean where we would hardly have bee
able to hear one another?'

'What I have to say…people around would hav
made it easier.'

Luiz was getting a nasty, unsettled feeling i
the pit of his stomach. She had turned him dow
once. It was something he hadn't forgotten. Thi
sounded very much like a second let-down an
he wasn't about to let that happen. Pride slamme
into him with the force of a sledgehammer.

'I'm getting the message that this *talk* of your
has to do with us?'

Aggie nodded miserably. This *talk* was some
thing she had rehearsed in her head for the pas

our hours and yet she was no closer to knowing where she would begin.

'What's there to talk about?' Luiz drawled grimly. 'We've already covered this subject. I'm not looking for commitment. Nor, you told me, were you. We understand one another. We're on the same page.'

'Sometimes things change.'

'Are you telling me that you're no longer satisfied with what we've got? That after a handful of weeks you're looking for something more?' Luiz refused to contemplate having his wings clipped. He especially didn't care for the thought of having anyone try to clip them on his behalf. Was she about to issue him with some kind of ultimatum? Promise more if he wanted to carry on seeing her, sleeping with her? Just thinking about it outraged him. Other women might have dropped hints—grown misty-eyed in front of jewellers, introduced him to friends with babies—but none of them had ever actually given him a stark choice and he was getting the feeling that that was precisely what Aggie was thinking of doing.

Aggie clenched her fists on her lap. The tone of his voice was like a slap in the face. Did he

really think that she had been stupid enough t
misunderstand his very clear ground rules?

'What if I were?' she asked, curious to se
where this conversation would take them, alread
predicting its final, painful destination and will
ing it masochistically on herself.

'Then I'd question whether you weren't won
dering if being married to a rich man might b
more financially lucrative than dating him!'

Every muscle in Aggie's body tensed and sh
looked at him astounded, hurt and horrified.

'How could you *say* that?'

Luiz scowled and looked away. He fully de
served that reprimand. He could scarcely cred
that he had actually accused her of having a fi
nancial agenda. She had proved to be one of th
least materialistic women he had ever met. Bu
hell, the thought of her walking out on him ha
sparked something in him he could barely unde
stand.

'I apologise,' he said roughly. 'That was belov
the belt.'

'But do you honestly believe it?' Aggie wa
driven to know whether this man she loved s
much could think so little of her that he actuall

hought she might try and con him into com-
nitment.

'No. I don't.'

She breathed a sigh of relief because she would
ever have been able to live with that.

'Then why did you say it?'

'Look, I don't know what this is about, but I'm
ot interested in playing games. And I won't have
ty hand forced. Not by you. Not by anybody.'

'Because you don't need anyone? The great
uiz Montes doesn't need anything or anyone!'

'And tell me, what's wrong with that?' He was
affled by her. Why the hell was she spoiling for
fight? And why had she suddenly decided that
he wanted more than what they had? Things
ad been pretty damn good between them. Bet-
er than good. He fought down the temptation to
xplode.

'I don't want to have this argument with you,'
ggie said, glancing towards the taxi driver who
vas maintaining a discreet disinterest. He prob-
bly heard this kind of thing all the time.

'And I don't want to argue with you,' Luiz con-
irmed smoothly. 'So why don't we pretend none
f it happened?' There was one way of stalling

any further confrontation. He pulled her toward
him and curled his hands into her soft hair.

Aggie's protesting hands against his ches
curved into an aching caress. As his tongu
delved to explore her mouth, she felt her body
come alive. Her nipples tightened in the lace bra
pushing forward in a painful need to be suckle
and touched. Her skin burned and the wetness be
tween her legs was an agonising reminder of how
this man could get to her. No matter that there
was talking to be done. No matter that making
love was not what she wanted to do.

'Now, isn't that better?' he murmured with sat
isfaction. 'I'd carry on, my darling, but I wouldn'
want to shock our cab driver.'

As if to undermine that statement, he curve
his hand over one full breast and slowly mas
saged it until she had to stop herself from cry
ing out.

Ever since they had begun seeing one another
her wardrobe had undergone a subtle transforma
tion. The uninspiring clothes she had worn ha
been replaced by a selection of brighter, mor
figure-hugging outfits.

'You're wearing a bra,' he chided softly into her ear. 'You know I hate that.'

'You can't always get what you want, Luiz.'

'But it's what we *both* want, isn't it? I get to touch you without the boring business of having to get rid of a bra and you get to be touched without the boring business of having to get rid of a bra. It's a win-win situation. Still, I guess sometimes it adds a little spice to the mix if I have to work my way through layers of clothes...'

'Stop it, Luiz!'

'Tell me you don't like what I'm doing.' He had shimmied his hand underneath the tight, striped jumper and had pulled down her bra to free one plump mound.

This was the way to stifle an argument, he thought. Maybe he had misread the whole thing. Maybe she hadn't been upping the ante. Maybe what she wanted to talk about had been altogether more prosaic. Luiz didn't know and he had no intention of revisiting the topic.

With a rueful sigh, he released her as the taxi slowed, moving into the crescent. He neatly pulled down the jumper, straightening it. 'Perhaps just as well that we're here,' he confessed

with a wicked glint in his dark eyes. 'Going al
the way in the back seat of a black cab would re
ally be taking things a step too far. I think whei
we get round to public performing we'll have to
think carefully where to begin...'

Aggie had had no intention of performing
with him on any level, never mind in public. Sh
shifted in the seat. When she should have beer
as cool as she could, she was hot and flustere
and having to push thoughts of him taking he
in his hallway out of her head.

The house which had once filled her with
awe she now appreciated in a distinctly les
gob-smacked way. She still loved the beautifu
objets d'art, but there were few personal touche
which made her think that money could buy som
things, but not others. It could buy beauty but nc
necessarily atmosphere. In fact, going out wit
Luiz had made her distinctly less cowed at th
impressive things money could buy and a lot les
daunted by the people who possessed it.

'So.' Luiz discarded his coat and jacket as soo
as they were through the door. 'Shall we fin
ish what we started? No need to go upstairs. I
you go right into the kitchen and sit on one c

the stools, I'll demonstrate how handy I can be with food. I guarantee I'll be a damn sight more imaginative with ingredients than that restaurant tonight was.'

'Luiz.' She was shaking as she placed her hand firmly on his chest. No giving in this time.

'Good God, woman! Tell me you don't want to start talking again.' He pushed his hands under her coat to cup her rounded buttocks, pulling her against him so that she could feel his arousal pushing through his trousers, as hard as a rod of iron. 'And, if you want to talk, then let's talk in bed.'

'Bed's not a good idea,' Aggie said shakily.

'Who says I want good ideas?'

'I'd like a cup of coffee.'

Luiz gave in with a groan of pure frustration. He banged his fist on the wall, shielded his head in the crook of his arm and then glanced at her with rueful resignation.

'Okay. You win. But take it from me, talking is never a very good idea.'

How true, Aggie thought. From his point of view, it would certainly not herald anything he wanted to hear.

She marvelled that in a few hours life could change so dramatically.

She had been poring over the school calendar and working out what lessons she should think about setting when something in her head had suddenly clicked.

She had seen the calendar and the concept of dates had begun to flicker. Dates of when she had last seen her period. She had never paid a great deal of attention to her menstrual cycle. It happened roughly on time. What more was there to say about it?

Her hands had been shaking when, a little over an hour later, she had taken that home-pregnancy test. She had already thought of a thousand reasons why she was silly to be concerned. For a start, Luiz was obsessive about contraception. Aside from that one little slip-up, he had been scrupulous.

Within minutes she had discovered how one little slip-up could change the course of someone's life.

She was pregnant by a man who didn't love her, had warned her off involvement and had certainly never expressed any desire to have chil dren. In the face of all those stark realities, she had briefly contemplated not telling him. Just breaking off the relationship; disappearing. Disappearing, she had reasoned for a few wild, disoriented moments, would not be difficult to do. She hated the house and her brother was soon to leave London to embark upon the next exciting phase of his life. She could ditch everything and return up north, find something there. Luiz would not pursue her and he would never know that he had fathered a child.

The thought didn't last long. He would find out; of course he would. Maria would tell him. And, aside from that, how could she deprive a man of his own child? Even a child he hadn't wanted?

'What I'm going to say will shock you,' Aggie told him as soon as they were sitting down in his living room, with a respectable distance between them.

Luiz, for the first time in his life, was prey to fear. It ripped through him, strangling his vocal chords, making him break out in a fine film of perspiration.

'You're not…ill, are you?'

Aggie looked at him with surprise. 'No. I'm

not,' she asserted firmly. He had visibly blanched and she knew why. Of course, he would be remembering his own father's illness, which he had spoken to her about in more depth over the time they had been together.

'Then what is it?'

'There's no easy way to tell you so I'm going to come right out and say it. I'm pregnant.'

Luiz froze. For a few seconds, he wondered whether he had heard correctly but he was not a man given to flights of imagination and the expression on her face was sufficient to tell him that she wasn't joking.

'You can't be,' he said eventually.

Aggie's eyes slid away from his. Whenever she had thought of being pregnant, it had been within a rosy scenario involving a man she loved who loved her back. Never had she envisaged breaking the news to a man who looked as though she had detonated a bomb in his front room.

'I'm afraid I can be, and I am.'

'I was careful!'

'There was that one time.' Against her better judgement—for she had hardly expected he news to be met with whoops of joy—she could feel a slow anger begin to burn inside her.

'You told me that there was no risk.'

'I'm sorry. I made a mistake.'

Luiz didn't say anything. He stood up and walked restively towards the floor-to-ceiling window to stare outside. The possibility of fatherhood was not one that had ever occurred to him. It was something that lay in the future. Way down the line. Possibly never. But she was carrying his baby inside her.

Aggie miserably looked at him, turned away from her and staring out of the window. Doubtless he was thinking about his life which now lay in ruins. If ever there was a man who was crushed under the weight of bad news, then he was that man.

'You decided to tell me this in a *pizzeria*?' Luiz spun round and walked towards her. He leaned over, bracing himself on either side of her, and Aggie shrank back into the chair.

'I didn't want…*this*!' she cried.

'This *what*?'

'I knew how you'd react and I thought it would

be more…more…civilised if I told you some
where out in the open!'

'What did you think I would do?'

'We need to discuss this like adults and we're
not going to get anywhere when you're standing
over me like this, threatening me!'

'God, how the hell did this happen?' Luiz re
turned to the sofa and collapsed onto it.

It felt to Aggie as though everything they had
shared had shattered under the blow of this preg
nancy. Which just went to show how fragile it
had all been from the very start. Not made to las
and not fashioned to withstand any knocks—al
though, in fairness, a pregnancy couldn't really
be called a knock. More like an earthquake, shak
ing everything from the foundations up.

'Stupid question.' He pressed his thumbs to hi
eyes and then leaned forward to look at her, hi
hands resting loosely on his thighs. 'Of course
I know how it happened, and you're right. We
have to talk about it. Hell, what's there to talk
about? We'll have to get married. What choice
do we have?'

'Get married? That's not what I want!' she
threw at him, fighting to contain her anger be

cause he was just doing what, in his misguided way, he construed as the decent thing. 'Do you really think I told you about this because I wanted you to marry me?'

'What does it matter? My family would be bitterly disappointed to think I had fathered a child and allowed it to be born out of wedlock.'

What a wonderful marriage proposal, Aggie thought with a touch of hysteria: *you're pregnant; we'd better get married or risk the wrath of my traditional family.*

'I don't think so,' Aggie said gently.

'What does that mean?'

'It means that I can't accept your generous marriage proposal.'

'Don't be crazy. Of course you can!'

'I have no intention of marrying someone just because I happen to be having his baby. Luiz, a pregnancy is not the right reason to be married to someone.' She could tell from the expression on his face that he was utterly taken aback that his offer had been rejected. 'I'm sorry if your parents would find it unacceptable for you to have a child out of wedlock, but I'm not going to marry you so that your parents can avoid disappointment.'

'That's not the only reason!'

'Well, what are the others?' She could quell the faint hope that he would say those three words she wanted to hear. That he loved her. He could expand on that. She wouldn't stop him. He could tell her that he couldn't live without her.

'It's better for a child to have both parents on hand. I am a rich man. I don't intend that any child of mine will go wanting. Two reasons and there's more!' Why, Luiz thought, was she being difficult? She had just brought his entire world crashing down around him and he had risen admirably to the occasion! Couldn't she see that?

'A child can have both parents on hand without them being married,' Aggie pointed out. 'I'm not going to deprive you of the opportunity to see him or her whenever you want, and of course I understand that you will want to assist financially. I would never dream of stopping you from doing that.' She lowered her eyes and nervously fiddled with her fingers.

There was something else that would have to be discussed. Would they continue to see one another? Part of her craved their ongoing relationship and the strength and support she would get from it. Another part realised that it would be foolhardy to carry on as though nothing had happened, as though a rapidly expanding stomach wasn't proof that their lives had changed for ever. She wouldn't marry him. She couldn't allow him to ruin his life for the sake of a gesture born from obligation. She hated the thought of what would happen as cold reality set in and he realised that he was stuck with her for good. He would end up hating and resenting her. He would seek solace in the arms of other women. He might even, one day, find a woman to truly love.

'And there's something else,' she said quietly. 'I don't think it's appropriate that we continue... seeing one another.'

'What?' Luiz exploded, his body alive with anger and bewilderment.

'Stop shouting!'

'Then don't give me a reason to shout!'

They stared at each other in silence. Aggie's heart was pounding inside her. 'What we have was never going to go the full distance. We both knew that. You were very clear on that.'

'Whoa! Before you get carried away with the

preaching, answer me this one thing. Do we o
do we not have fun when we're together?' Lui
felt as though he had started the evening witl
clear skies and calm seas, only to discover tha
a force-ten hurricane had been waiting just ove
the horizon. Not only had he found himself with
baby on the way, but on top of that here she was
informing him that she no longer wanted to hav
anything to do with him. A growing sense o
panicked desperation made him feel slightly ill

'That's not the point!'

'Then what the hell is? You're not making an
sense, Aggie! I've offered to do the right thing
by you and you act as though I've insulted you
You rumble on about a child not being a goo
enough reason for us to be married. I don't ge
it! Not only is a child a bloody good reason t
get married, but here's the added bonus—we'r
good together! But that's not enough for you
Now, you're talking about walking away from
this relationship!'

'We're friends at the moment and that's hov
I'd like our relationship to stay for the sake o
our child, Luiz.'

'We're more than just friends, damn it!'

'We're friends with benefits.'

'I can't believe I'm hearing this!' He slashed the air with his hand in a gesture of frustration, incredulity and impatience. His face was dark with anger and those beautiful eyes that could turn her hot and cold were flat with accusation.

In this sort of mood, withstanding him was like trying to swim up a waterfall. Aggie wanted to fly to him and just let him decide what happened next. She knew it would be a mistake. If they carried on seeing one another and reached the point where, inevitably, he became fed up and bored, their relationship thereafter would be one of bitterness and discomfort. Couldn't he see long-term? For a man who could predict trends and work out the bigger picture when it came to business, he was hopelessly inadequate in doing the same when it came to his private life. He lived purely for the moment. Right now he was living purely for the moment with her and he wasn't quite ready for it to end. Right now, his solution to their situation was to put a ring on her finger, thereby appeasing family and promoting his sense of responsibility. He just didn't think ahead.

Aggie knew, deep down, that if she didn't love him she would have accepted that marriage proposal. She would not have invested her emotions in a hopeless situation. She would have been able to see their union as an arrangement that made sense and would have been thankful that he was standing by her. Was it any wonder that he was now looking at her as though she had taken leave of her senses?

'I don't want us to carry on, waiting until the physical side of things runs out of steam and you start looking somewhere else,' she told him bluntly. 'I don't want to become so disillusioned with you that I resent you being in my life. I wouldn't be a good background for a child.'

'Who says the physical side would run out of steam?'

'It always has for you! Hasn't it? Unless…I'm different? Unless what you feel for me is…different?'

Suddenly feeling cornered, Luiz fell back on the habits of a lifetime of not yielding to leading questions. 'You're having my baby. Of course you're different.'

'I'm beginning to feel tired, Luiz.' Aggie won

ered why she continued to hope for words that
weren't going to come. 'And you've had a shock.
I think we both need to take a little time out to
think about things, and when we next meet we
can discuss the practicalities.'

'The practicalities...?' Luiz was finding it hard
to get a grip on events.

'You've been nagging me to move out of that
house.' Aggie smiled wryly. 'I guess that might
be something on the list to discuss.' She stood
up to head for her coat and he stilled her with
his hand.

'I don't want you going back to that place tonight. Or ever. It's disgusting. You have my baby
to consider now.'

'And that's the word, Luiz—*discuss*. Which
doesn't mean you tell me what you want me to
do and I obey.'

She began putting on her coat while Luiz
watched with the feeling that she was slipping
through his fingers.

'You're making a mistake,' he ground out, bar-
ing her exit and staring down at her.

'I think,' Aggie said sadly, 'the mistakes have
already been made.'

CHAPTER TEN

LUIZ looked at the pile of reports lying on his desk eagerly awaiting his attention and swivelled his chair round to face the expanse of glass that overlooked the busy London streets several stories below.

It was another one of those amazing spring days: blue, cloudless skies, a hint of a breeze. It did nothing to improve his concentration levels. Or his mood, for that matter. Frankly, his mood was in urgent need of improvement ever since Aggie had announced her pregnancy over two months ago.

For the first week, he had remained convinced that she would come to her senses and accept his offer of marriage. He had argued for it from a number of fronts. He had demanded that she give him more good reasons why she couldn't see it from his point of view. It had been as successful as beating his head against a brick wall.

It had seemed to him, in his ever-increasing frustration, that the harder he tried to push the faster she retreated, so he had dropped the subject and they had discussed all those practicalities she had talked about.

At least there she had listened to what he had to say and agreed with pretty much everything. At least her pride wasn't going to let her get in the way of accepting the massively generous financial help he had insisted on providing, although she had stopped short of letting him buy her the house of her dreams.

'When I move into my dream house,' she had told him, her mouth set in a stubborn line, 'I don't want to know that it's been bought for me as part of a package deal because I happen to be pregnant.'

But she had moved out of the hovel two weeks previously, into a small, modern box in a pleasant part of London close to her job. The job which he insisted she would carry on doing until she no longer could, despite his protests that there was no need, that she had to look after herself.

'I'm more than happy to accept financial help as far as the baby is concerned,' she had told him firmly. 'But there's no need for you to lump me in the same bracket.'

'You're the mother of my child. Of course I'm going to make sure that you get all the money you need.'

'I'm not going to be dependent on you, Luiz. I intend to carry on working until I have the baby and then I shall take it up again as soon as I feel the baby is old enough for a nursery. The hours are good at the school and there are all the holidays. It's a brilliant job to have if you've got a family.'

Luiz loathed the thought of that just as he loathed the fact that she had managed to shut him out of her life. They communicated, and there were no raised voices, but she had withdrawn from him and it grated on him, made him ill-tempered at work, incapable of concentrating.

And now something else had descended to prey on his mind. It was a thought that had formulated a week ago when she had mentioned in passing that she would be going to the spring party which all the teachers had every year.

Somehow, he had contrived to ignore the fact that she had a social life outside him. Re-

ninded of it, he had quizzed her on what her
ellow teachers were like, and had discovered
nat they weren't all female and they weren't all
niddle-aged. They enjoyed an active social life.
'he teaching community was close-knit, with
nany teachers from different schools socialis-
ng out of work.

'You're pregnant,' he had informed her. 'Par-
es are a no-go area.'

'Don't worry. I won't be drinking,' she had
nughed, and right then he had had a worrying
nought.

She had turned down his marriage proposal,
ad put their relationship on a formal basis, and
'as this because she just wanted to make sure
nat she wasn't tied down? Had he been sidelined
ecause at the back of her mind, baby or no baby,
ne wanted to make sure that she could return
o an active social life? One that involved other
nen, the sort of men she was normally drawn
o? He had been an aberration. Was she eager to
esume relationships with one of those creative
ypes who weren't mired in work and driven by
mbition?

Luiz thought of the reports waiting on his desk

and smiled sardonically. If only she knew... No one could accuse him of being mired in work now, or driven by ambition. Having a bomb detonate in his life had certainly compelled him to discover the invaluable art of delegation! If only his mother could see him now, she would be overjoyed that work was no longer the centre of his universe.

A call interrupted the familiar downward trend of his thoughts and he took it on the second ring.

He listened, scribbled something on a piece of paper and stood up.

For the first time in weeks, he felt as though he was finally doing something; finally, for better or for worse, trying to stop a runaway train which was what his life had become.

Over the weeks, his secretary had grown so accustomed to her boss's moody unpredictability—a change from the man whose life had previously been so highly organised—that she nodded without question when he told her that he would be going out and wasn't sure when he would be back. She had stopped pointing out meetings that required his presence. Her brain now moved into another gear, the one which had her immediately working out who would replace him.

Luiz called his driver on his way down. Aggie would be at school. He tried to picture her expression when he showed up. It distracted him from more tumultuous thoughts—thoughts of her having his child and then rediscovering a single life; thoughts of her getting involved with another man; thoughts of that other man bringing up his, Luiz's, child as his own while Luiz was relegated to playing second fiddle. The occasional father.

Having never suffered the trials and tribulations of a fertile imagination, he found that he had more than made up for the lifelong omission. Now, his imagination seemed to be a monstrous thing released from a holding pen in which it had been imprisoned for its entire life, and now it was making up for lost time.

It was a situation that Luiz could not allow to continue but, as the car wound its way through traffic that was as dense as treacle, he was gripped by a strange sense of panic. He had spent all of his adult life knowing where he was going, knowing how he was going to get there. Recently, the signposts had been removed and the road

was no longer a straight one forward. Instead,
curved in all directions and he had no idea wher
he would end up. He just knew the person h
wanted to find at its destination.

'Can't you go a little faster?' he demanded, an
cursed silently when his driver shot him a jaun
diced look in the rear-view mirror before poin
ing out that they hadn't yet invented a car tha
could fly—although, when and if they ever dic
he was sure that Mr Montes would be the firs
to own one.

They made it to the school just as the be
sounded for lunch and Aggie was heading to th
staff room. She had been blessed with an ab
sence of morning sickness but she felt tired a lc
of the time.

And it was such a struggle maintaining a dis
tance from Luiz. Whenever she heard that deer
dark drawl down the end of the telephone, ask
ing her how her day had been, insisting she tel
him everything she had done, telling her abou
what he had done, she wanted nothing more tha
to take back everything she had said about nc
wanting him in her life. He phoned a lot. He vis
ited a lot. He treated her like a piece of delicat

china, and when she told him not to he shrugged his shoulders ruefully and informed her that he couldn't help being a dinosaur when it came to stuff like that.

She had thought when she had delivered her speech to him all those weeks ago that he would quickly come to terms with the fact that he would not be shackled to her for the wrong reasons. She had thought that he would soon begin to thank her for letting him off the hook, that he would begin to relish his freedom. An over-developed sense of responsibility was something that wouldn't last very long. He didn't love her. It would be easy for him to cut the strings once he had been given permission to do so.

But he wasn't making it easy for her to get over him. Or to move on.

She had now moved from the dump, as he had continued to call it, and was happy enough in the small, modern house he had provided for her. She was still in her job and had insisted that she would carry on working before and after the baby was born, but there were times when she longed to be away from London with its noise, pollution and traffic.

And, aside from those natural doubts, she was plagued by worries about how things would unravel over time.

She couldn't envisage ever seeing him without being affected. Having been so convinced that she was doing the right thing in refusing to marry him, having prided herself on her cool ability to look at the bigger picture, she found herself riddled with angst that she might have made the wrong decision.

She stared with desolation at the sandwich she had brought in with her and was about to bite into it when…there he was.

Amid the chaos of children running in the corridors and teachers moving around the school stopping to tell them off, Luiz was suddenly in front of her, lounging against the door to the staff room.

'I know you don't like me coming here,' Luiz greeted her as he strolled towards her desk. He wondered whether she should be eating more than just a sandwich for her lunch but refrained from asking.

'You always cause such a commotion,' Aggie said honestly. 'What do you want, anyway?

have a lot of work to do during my lunch hour. I can't take time out.'

As always, she had to fight the temptation to touch him. It was as though, whenever she saw him, her brain sent signals to her fingers, making them restive at remembered pleasures. He always looked so good! Too good. His hair had grown and he hadn't bothered to cut it and the slight extra length suited him, made him even more outrageously sexy. Now he had perched on the side of her table and she had to drag her eyes away from the taut pull of his trousers over his muscular thighs.

Luiz watched as she looked away, eager for him to leave, annoyed that he had shown up at her workplace. Tough. He couldn't carry on as he had. He was going crazy. There were things he needed to say to her and, the further she floated away from him, the more redundant his words would become.

Teachers were drifting in now, released from their classes by the bell, and Luiz couldn't stop himself from glancing at them, trying to see whether any of the men might be contenders for Aggie. There were three guys so far, all in their thirties from the looks of it, but surely none of them would appeal to her?

Once, he would have been arrogantly certain of his seductive power over her. Unfortunately, he was a lot less confident on that score, and he scowled at the thought that some skinny guy with ginger hair might become his replacement.

'You look tired,' Luiz said abruptly.

'Have you come here to do a spot check on me? I wish you'd stop clucking over me like a mother hen, Luiz. I told you I can take care of myself and I can.'

'I haven't come here to do a spot check on you.'

'Then why are you here?' She risked a look at him and was surprised at the hesitation on his face.

'I want to take you somewhere. I… There are things I need to…talk to you about.'

Instinctively, Aggie knew that whatever he wanted to talk about would not involve finances, the baby or her health—all of which were subjects he covered in great detail in his frequent visits—whilst, without even being aware of it, continuing to charm her with witty anecdotes of what he was up to and the people he met. S

hat, she wondered nervously, could be impor-
nt enough for him to interrupt her working day
nd to put such a hesitant expression on his usu-
lly confident face?

All at once her imagination took flight. There
as no doubt that he was getting over her. He
ad completely stopped mentioning marriage. In
ict, she hadn't heard a word on the subject for
eeks. He visited a lot and phoned a lot but she
new that that was because of the baby she was
arrying. He was an 'all or nothing' man. Having
ever contemplated the thought of fatherhood,
e had had it foisted upon him and had reacted
y embracing it with an enthusiasm that was so
pical of his personality. He did nothing in half-
leasures.

As the woman who happened to be carrying
is child, she was swept up in the tidal wave of
is enthusiasm. But already she could see the
igns of a man who no longer viewed her with
le untrammelled lust he once had. He could see
er so often and speak to her so often because
he had become *a friend*. She no longer stirred
is passion.

Aggie knew that she should have been happy

about this because it was precisely what she ha
told him, at the beginning, was necessary fo
their relationship to survive on a long-term basi
Friendship and not lust would be the key to th
sort of amicable union they would need to b
good parents to their child.

Where he had taken that on board, however, sh
was still struggling and now she couldn't thin
what he might want to talk to her about that ha
necessitated a random visit to the school.

Could it be that he had found someone else
That would account for the shadow of uncei
tainty on his face. Luiz was not an uncertai
man. Fear gripped her, turning her complexio
chalky white. She could think of no other rea
son for him to be here and to want to *have a tai*
with her. A talk that was so urgent it couldn
wait. He intended to brace her for the news be
fore she heard about it via the grapevine, for he
brother would surely find out and impart the in
formation to her.

'Is it about…financial stuff?' she asked, cling
ing to the hope that he would say yes.

'It's nothing to do with money, or with an
practicalities, Aggie. My car's outside.'

Aggie nodded but her body was numb all over as she gathered her things, her bag, her lightweight jacket and followed him to where his car was parked on a single yellow line outside the school.

'Where are we going? I have to be back at school by one-thirty.'

'You might have to call and tell them that you'll be later.'

'Why? What can you have to say that can't be said closer to the school? There's a café just down that street ahead. Let's go there and get this little talk of yours over and done with.'

'It's not that easy, I'm afraid.'

She noticed that the hesitation was back and it chilled her once again to the core.

'I'm stronger than you think,' she said, bracing herself. 'I can handle whatever you have to tell me. You don't need to get me to some fancy restaurant to break the news.'

'We're not going to a fancy restaurant. I know you well enough by now not to make the mistake of taking you somewhere fancy unless you have at least an hour to get ready in advance.'

'It's not my fault I still get a little nervous at

some of those places you've taken me to. I don't feel comfortable being surrounded by celebrities!'

'And it's what I like about you,' Luiz murmured. That, along with all the thousands of other little quirks which should have shown him by now the significance of what he felt for her. He had always counted himself as a pretty shrewd guy and yet, with her, he had been as thick as the village idiot.

'It is?' Aggie shamefully grasped that barely audible compliment.

'I want to show you something.' The traffic was free-flowing and they were driving quickly out of London now, heading towards the motorway. For a while, Aggie's mind went into freefall as she recollected the last time she had been in a car heading out of London. His car. Except then the snow had been falling thick and fast and little had she known that she had been heading towards a life-changing destiny. If, at the time, she had been in possession of a crystal ball, would she have looked into it and backed away from sleeping with him? The answer, of course, was no. For better or for worse she had thought at the

ime, and she still thought so now, even though
he better had lasted for precious little time.

'What?' Aggie pressed anxiously.

'You'll have to wait and see.'

'Where are we going?'

'Berkshire. Close enough. We'll be there shortly.'

Aggie fell silent but her mind continued play-
ng with a range of ever-changing worst-case sce-
narios, yet she couldn't imagine what he could
possibly have to show her outside London. She
hadn't thought there was much outside the city
that interested him although, to be fair, whenever
he spoke of his time spent on that fateful journey,
his voice held a certain affection for the places
they had seen.

She was still trying to work things out when
the car eventually pulled up in front of a sprawl-
ng field and he reached across to push open the
door for her.

'What…what are we doing here?' She looked at
him in bewilderment and he urged her out, leading her across the grass verge and into the field
which, having been reached via a series of twist-
ing, small lanes, seemed to be surrounded by

nothing. It was amazing, considering they were still so close to London.

'Do you like it?' Luiz gazed down at her as she mulled over his question.

'It's a field, Luiz. It's peaceful.'

'You don't like me buying you things,' he murmured roughly. 'You have no idea how hard it is for me to resist it but you've made me see that there are other ways of expressing…what I feel for you. Hell, Aggie. I don't know if I'm telling you this the way I should. I'm no good at…things like this—talking about feelings.'

Aggie stared up at his perfect face, shadowed with doubt and strangely vulnerable. 'What are you trying to say?'

'Something I should have said a long time ago.' He looked down at her and shuffled awkwardly. 'Except I barely recognised it myself, until you turned me away. Aggie, I've been going crazy. Thinking about you. Wanting you. Wondering how I'm going to get through life without you. I don't know if I've left it too late, but I can't live without you. I need you.'

Buffeted in all directions by wonderful waves of hope, Aggie could only continue to stare. She

was finding it hard to make the necessary connections. Caution was pleading with her not to
jump to conclusions but the look in his eyes was
filling her with burgeoning, breathless excitement.

Luiz stared into those perfect blue eyes and
took strength from them.

'I don't know what you feel for me,' he said
huskily. 'I turned you on but that wasn't enough.
When it came to women, I wasn't used to deal-
ing in any other currency aside from sex. How
was I to know that what I felt for you went far
beyond lust?'

'When you say *far beyond...*'

'I don't know when I fell in love with you,
but I did and, fool that I am, it's been a realisation that's been long in coming. I can only hope
not too long. Look, Aggie...' He raked long fingers through his hair and shook his head in the
manner of someone trying hard to marshal his
thoughts into coherent sentences. 'I'm taking the
biggest gamble of my life here, and hoping that
I haven't blown all my chances with you. I love
you and...I want to marry you. We were happy
once, we had fun. You may not love me now, but

I swear to God I have enough love for the two of us and one day you'll come to…'

'Shh.' She placed a finger over his beautiful mouth. 'Don't say another word.' Tears trembled glazing over her eyes. 'I turned down your marriage proposal because I couldn't cope with the thought that the man I was…*am*…desperately in love with had only proposed because he thought it was the thing he should do. I couldn't face the thought of a reluctant, resentful husband. It would have meant my heart breaking every day we were together and that's why I turned you down.' She removed her finger and tiptoed to lightly kiss his lips.

'You'll marry me?'

Aggie smiled broadly and fell into him, reaching up to link her hands behind his neck. 'It's been agony seeing you and talking to you,' she confessed. 'I kept wondering if I had done the right thing.'

'Well, it's good to hear that I wasn't the only one suffering.'

'So you brought me all the way out here to tell me that you love me?'

'To show you this field and hope that it could be my strongest argument to win you back.'

'What do you mean?'

'Like I said.' Luiz, with his arm around her shoulders, turned her so that they were both looking at the same sprawling vista of grass and trees. 'I know you don't like me buying you things so I bought this for us. Both of us.'

'You bought...this field?'

'Thirty acres of land with planning permission to build. There are strict guidelines on what we can build but we can design it together. This was going to be my last attempt to prove to you that I was no longer the arrogant guy you once couldn't stand, that I could think out of the box, that I was worth the gamble.'

'My darling.' Aggie turned to him. 'I love you so much.' There was so much more she wanted to say but she was so happy, so filled with joy that she could hardly speak.

* * * * *

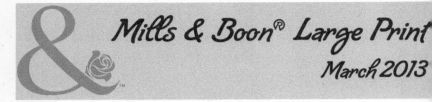

Mills & Boon® Large Print
March 2013

A NIGHT OF NO RETURN
Sarah Morgan

A TEMPESTUOUS TEMPTATION
Cathy Williams

BACK IN THE HEADLINES
Sharon Kendrick

A TASTE OF THE UNTAMED
Susan Stephens

THE COUNT'S CHRISTMAS BABY
Rebecca Winters

HIS LARKVILLE CINDERELLA
Melissa McClone

THE NANNY WHO SAVED CHRISTMAS
Michelle Douglas

SNOWED IN AT THE RANCH
Cara Colter

EXQUISITE REVENGE
Abby Green

BENEATH THE VEIL OF PARADISE
Kate Hewitt

SURRENDERING ALL BUT HER HEART
Melanie Milburne

0213 Rom LP

Mills & Boon® Large Print
April 2013

A TEMPESTUOUS
TEMPTATION